# THE
# GOOD
# SAMARITAN

*Dan Brizzee*

# DAN BRIZZEE

PAGE PUBLISHING
Conneaut Lake, PA

First originally published by Page Publishing 2024

ISBN 979-8-89157-931-6 (pbk)
ISBN 979-8-89157-954-5 (digital)

Printed in the United States of America

# The Graduation Party

John Blackwell was a tennis champ at UCLA, but he was a much bet-ter boxer. He graduated with a PhD in math and physics. He wasn't Jewish, but his mother was. He didn't know his father, and it is sup-posed that was the reason that he and his mother were treated as out-casts. He refused the faith, and perhaps that was the reason he found himself on the outs with that religion. However, his mother was per-sistent, and at his graduation, she brought him a trip to Europe for thirty-six months and a nice Jewish woman to meet. The woman was the daughter of a high-finance banker in San Francisco.

He thought, *What can an engineer do at a bank?*

They finished dinner with some kind of desert. They had coffee and brandy in the enclosed veranda. Wanda, that was the name of the woman, was chomping at the bit. She snuggled up next to Jack in a love seat. Mother went to schmooze with some of the highbrow guests.

Jack felt rather strange because he was used to younger college girls. They didn't understand most of their conversations. He wasn't sure what was proper in this circumstance. So he turned and looked her up and down but said nothing.

Wanda quipped, "Well, do I meet with your approval?"

Jack chortled. "What are you talking about?"

"Well, I have all the parts it takes. I admit, I'm a little heavy, and my hair isn't so great. My hips are wide, as you could see when I came over to sit by you, but I know what goes where and why." She leaned into him and whispered, "Let's get away from here. Take me someplace exciting. Get me voluptuous. There may be reward."

He turned to face her directly. "What is your scheme?" he groused.

She licked her lower lip. "We could have such fun. I've heard you can be exciting," she whimpered. She turned and looked back to the party.

Spying his mother, she cried, "Oh, look! Your mother isn't paying any attention to us. Let's skedaddle while the coast is clear. Your mother won't mind. Can you call for a cab?"

"I know just the place. Do you have a wrap?"

"No, just this light top jacket. Look, wave to your mom. Isn't she smiling?"

They ambled through the revolving door. He let her go out ahead of him. He thought she would turn around and wait for him. She sure did. He got a very good look at her. He stopped the door, just to look at her. She was hippy but workable. Her hair was like a page boy, with a slight curl at the end. Very plain—a roman nose and rather thin lips with too much lipstick— but she might be worth a tumble. When he came through the door, she grabbed his arm and hung on him like she would never let go. He tried to hail a cab but failed.

She said, "Watch this." She gave out a whistle so loud that everyone turned and looked at her.

The cab came up rubbing the curb of the sidewalk. Jack opened the door, and she jumped in. He slid in beside her, pulling the door closed as he did.

He sat back and said, "Columbus and Vine, Trav Lye."

Cabbie replied, "Yeah, Mac, I know the place. That's in North Beach, right?"

Jack jibbed, "Yeah, it's past uptown."

Wanda quipped, "Leave the cabbie alone. He knows the way. I want some attention on the way.

"How about a snuggle and some cuddling? Wouldn't that be called for or nice?"

She quipped, "Well, when you come on, you come on."

"Well, come on."

They played all the way to the club.

The cabbie said, "Break it up. We're here—Trav Lye. That'll be $1.65."

Jack handed him a five and said, "Keep the change."

Wanda was getting herself back together. "I just need to put on my face."

Cabbie said, "I'm off duty. I'll have a cup of coffee and a smoke. Your fella finished my day."

# THE GREAT SHOW

Jack called, "Hey, Wanda, the last show is about to start, so slide over here, and let's get in there before they dim the lights."

As she slid over to the passenger door, the seat cover caused her skirt to hike up and exposed her garter belt and her fleshy white inner thigh. She let it be, gave her hand to Jack, and he lifted her out and onto the sidewalk.

She took his arm, and pulling herself up into him, she whispered, "That little peek was done on purpose."

He said to himself, *She is really chomping at the bit. I wonder how old she is. I'll find out on the way back to her place.*

They rushed into the club and were shown to their seat, which was actually a booth. He ordered tea and baklava. The lights went down, and the dancer appeared and began her routine of typical belly dancer, moving around to every table. The lights went down again, and when they came back up, the same woman danced on a stage in the middle of the floor, which was only about a foot in height. She stood facing to the side of the room where there were no tables. She began bending over backward until her hands rested on the stage where she stood. She began drawing her feet and ankles under herself until her lower buttocks rested on the heels of her feet. That was all performed in a bright light. The light continued so that the next part

4

of the performance could be appreciated. A female attendant attired in the same garb appeared, carrying ten silver dollars, and proceeded to place each dollar in the indentations between the muscles of her abdomen. The attendant disappeared. At first, the dancer turned the entire row of silver dollars, laying them all down toward her pelvis, then standing them back up again, then laying them all toward her navel. Then the most incredible feat was when she began to lay each and every one of them individually, back and forth, and finally, she had them going back and forth until it seemed like a domino setup. The attendant appeared and began picking up the silver dollars, but the dancer would move them as the attendant was attempting to snatch the dollar, only to have it moved away, but eventually, they were all confiscated, and the dancer began to gyrate and began to emerge as if she were coming out of an eggshell to a standing position. Then she began to continue dancing to each table, and the male guests were encouraged to slip folding currency as deep into her bikini-type bottom as they dared. When she came to Jack, he laid a five-dollar bill in his palm and held it with his thumb. And when he slipped the bill down until the key was the only part that was showing, he felt nothing but smooth skin.

The dancer said, "I can't give change." Everybody laughed.

Wanda raised her eyebrows and gibed, "See, I knew that you weren't afraid of women."

He pursed his lips and chortled. "I can take them or leave them."

She made a pouty lip and quipped, "Does that mean that I don't have a chance?"

"I didn't say anything about a chance, but with a great deal of effort, I am sure that I could be influenced."

The pastry was gone, and the tea was cool, so they made their way out the front door and onto the sidewalk. Wanda spotted a cab up the street and gave out a whistle. Fortunately, the cab was already moving toward them but sped up and came to a stop right in front of them. Jack pulled the door and swung it open, and Wanda hopped in, and as Jack climbed in, he pulled the door behind himself.

Sitting down against Wanda, he said, "Ten Union, Benton Heights."

5

Wanda piped up, "Let us know when you get to Palo Alto. Until then, keep your rearview mirror turned up."

The cabbie replied, "That is quite a way." He flipped up the rearview mirror. "Say, are you the couple that closed the Trav Lye club?"

Jack quipped, "It was just a great show."

# PLEASE STEP OFF

Wanda gibed, "Can we go now?" Slipping off her light jacket, she began unbuttoning her white blouse and quipped, "A penny for your thoughts."

He looked at her plainness, her tendering—all she does for acceptance. He looked at her face and said, "No, stop. This is not what I want."

She scowled and asked, "Well, what do you want?"

"First, I must ask. What is your age?"

She smiled a weak smile and chortled. "Well, I'm over eighteen. Why do you ask?"

He raised his eyebrows and quizzed, "How old are you?"

She looked out the window, at the city going by, and quipped, "If you must know, I'll be twenty-six next October. Does this disqualify me?"

He thought, *I better say something, but I don't know what.* He looked at the dome light and quipped, "That all depends on what kind of relationship you want us to have."

She felt like a deer in the headlights, but she droned, "What do you think?" She wanted to grovel, but she was afraid that if she did and he turned her down, she might be relegated to being a spinster, living off her father's money. But what if he just dropped her off at her place and disappeared?

He looked out the window and said, "There is Morgan Hill." He just kept looking without speaking.

She squeezed his thigh and groaned, "I'll make you happy, no matter what it takes." She laid her head against his chest and looked up at him.

With tears in her eyes, he pushed her away so that she sat up. He looked at her, and all he saw was a mound of flesh. He wanted to take advantage of her right then, and she would've pulled him in with delight, but they would be stuck in a malaise of ill feelings.

He pulled her head back by her hair and said, "This is all you're going to get from me." He kissed her hard and long—ah, French. He felt her hot breath, and their eyes flashed open. He let her down.

The cab sat in front of her place. He made her get out on her own. She stopped twice on the walkway to her front door. Lights lit up along the walk, and a light came from inside the doorway.

He leaned back in the seat and said, "Let's go."

The cab drove away.

The cabbie asked, "What's the destination? I feel sorry for that girl. Why were you so mean?"

Jack chuckled and quipped, "I had to be firm. She was trying to trap me. Her daddy will get her married off to some immigrant from Holland or some little country, and the guy will be working in her daddy's bank. She will get what she wants but probably not what she deserves. Let's pick up my mom in Oakland, and then she and I will catch the Santa Fe to LA. You will get paid plenty and go home happy. So drive on."

Waiting for the LA Limited at the station, Jack put their luggage on the carrier and said, "Mama, please, don't set me up anymore."

Mama twisted in her seat and said, "Why, what is wrong with that girl? She is nice, and she is from a good family. And did you see those hips? She could have babies like popcorn."

"Mama, she is a hussy."

Mama stood up and said, "Maybe you're right. I don't want grandchildren that bad. Besides, maybe you will bring home a nice Jewish girl from Austria."

# The Santa Fe Out of LA

He tried to stay out of sight into Los Angeles, traveling south at night. The interior of the car was passable in temperature, but he knew that as soon as the train drove south into the desert route, the metal in the cars would begin to heat up, and in 1935, there was no air-conditioning. And a fan would only blow hot air. He was awakened by a bright complete sunrise. He could feel the heat of the day beginning. He arose and got dressed to go for breakfast. He bought a paper as the waiter showed him to his table. As they passed the rows of tables, he noticed that all the tables were taken by two people, except the one at the very end, and that table had one occupant.

The waiter ushered him to that table, but the occupant, said, "I asked for a table alone."

Jack, taken back, said, "Well, that is not very amicable, and I'm not disposed to sit here after all."

The occupant, spying his newspaper, jacket, and tie, recanted her complaint, saying, "Perhaps, a little conversation is just may be what I need."

Jack scoffed, sitting down, tossed the newspaper on the table. "Well, you changed your mind quickly."

She threw her head back and laughed. "Yes, I am a quick wit, aren't I?"

He unfolded the newspaper and asked, "Which section do you want?"

She leaned forward to see and said, "The only part I read is the comics." She spotted the comics and pulled them free and asked, "Are you a college graduate or something? I mean, because you use those big words."

He leaned his section forward and said, "Yeah, something like that. How far did you get in school?"

She folded the comics in half and said, "I almost went to college, but I wasn't smart enough. Say, how old are you anyway?"

"I'm twenty-four. How about you? Age, I mean."

She turned a page of the comics and said, "I'll be thirty-seven in July, I think. Say, what is the date anyhow?"

He looked up to one side of the front page and said, "It is April 10, 1935." He pulled the newspaper together and said, "I came over here to have breakfast. Where is that waiter? Have you had breakfast?"

She grimaced and said, "No, it isn't in my budget."

He clinched his lips and said, "I'll take care of that. Do you take coffee or tea?" He surmised she wasn't Jewish.

She cleared her throat and said, "How very kind of you. Thank you. Coffee, please."

He looked at her hand. Her skin looked soft. "We'll see."

She looked in his eyes and smiled. Breakfast came. She took a napkin and wiped the lipstick from her lips. They began to eat.

He leaned forward. "I have a chess set in my cabin. Do you care to play?"

"When we finish breakfast and coffee, should I reapply my lipstick?"

He rubbed his chin and smiled. "That is up to you."

She dropped her lipstick tube into her purse. Then lifting the coffeepot and shaking it, she said, "There's another cup. Shall we split it?"

"Sure." He spoke. She poured the coffee.

He took a sip and said, "I don't know your name, and you don't know my name. Should we introduce ourselves?"

She said, "My name is Hellen."

He said, "I'm Jack." They finished their coffee.

Hellen said, "I don't know how to play chess."

He tapped the edge of the folded-up newspaper on the table. "Perhaps we will find something to amuse ourselves in my cabin." He stood and extended his hand to her, to help her up.

She accepted, and taking his hand, she rose, saying, "I'm sure we will find some sort of amusement."

Jack led her down a hallway, with the cabins on one side and windows with the scenery going by on the other. He unlocked the sliding pocket door, and sliding it open, he motioned for her to enter. He followed her in and slid the door closed.

She stepped to the window, with the world going by on the other side of the cabin. Then she turned, looking at the furnishings, then at Jack. "This is just swell, but will I get in trouble if I'm caught in here?"

"You're my guest. This cabin is meant to accommodate two people, and it is already paid for."

Hellen noticed a small love seat close to the vanity and asked, "Can we sit down?"

"Of course. Have a seat."

She looked down and asked, "Do you think it will hold me? I weigh 130 pounds. It looks a little small."

"I weigh more than that, and I sit in it every morning when I tie my shoes."

"Okay, you allowed it." She eased into the seat. "Is there enough room for you?"

"Of course, that is why it is called a love seat. We are going to be close."

He sat down, and they were against each other. He put his arm around her and pulled her to him and said, "Isn't this cozy?"

"Yes, would you like to kiss me now?" she whispered.

He said, "When you come on, you come on."

She looked up and said, "Well, come on."

They shared a kiss, but it was soon accompanied by an embrace. He gave her a final tender squeeze and leaned back on the arm of the love seat.

She turned her back to him and said, "Would you like to cuddle?" She already began unbuttoning the top of her dress.

He turned her around and said, "I would rather ask you what you would like."

She lowered her head in humility and said, "I would like to take off my shoes, but I am afraid that the smell would be terrible. My feet are so sore. I need to wash them, but I have no place to do it."

He stood up, pulled off his jacket, and undid his tie. Cuff links went on the vanity; he took off his shirt and laid it on one of the beds. From under the vanity, he produced a shallow basin and a clean towel. He knelt down in front of her and said, "Let me have your shoes."

"I can't get my dress wet," she complained. She stood while she completed to unbutton her dress and laid it next to his shirt laying on the bed, then returned to the love seat, pulling her slip up out of the way, and sat down straddling the basin.

She leaned forward and said, "Now are you sure about this?"

He dipped the washcloth in the warm water and rolled a cake of soap in it. He began washing, even between her toes. She jerked a couple of times because she got tickled. Soon, they were dried off and squeaky-clean.

He looked up, and big tears were falling from her eyes. He asked, "Why those big tears? Isn't that better?"

"My tears are not because of my feet. My tears are because I know I could never have a husband like you."

"Not me, but I have plans for you. We can still give each other solace and succor together."

Taking the basin in hand, he stood and emptied the basin into the sink. He glanced at her as he stepped back, picking up the washcloth and towel, then simultaneously dropped them into the laundry chute. He turned, looking at her, and said, "Are we better now?"

Standing up, she said, "I'm better, but I don't think I'll ever be whole ever again. Will you hold me for a while?"

He held out his arms to her and said, "Come here."

She stepped closer, and he pulled her close and tight, wrapping her in his arms. She put her arm around his waist and caressed his neck, with her other hand. She held her face against his face and said, "I have to tell you something. I want to tell you something."

He tilted his head back and asked, "What?"

She laid her head on his shoulder and asked, "Will you continue holding me while I tell you? Because I can't face you to tell you."

Looking straight ahead, he said, "I'll hold you as long as you want."

She began to sob softly. He pulled his T-shirt up to wipe her nose. She leaned back, looking up at him, then laid her head against his chest. She breathed deeply a couple of times. Then silence followed, but he didn't mind. She felt so good in his arms. She cleared her throat and spoke. "Do you remember when we met and I wanted to be alone? Well, the reason I wanted to be alone was because I was hatching a plan to get out of my troubles. Hold me closer, please. You know, I got on the train in Los Angeles, but you didn't know that my destination is Miami. The reason my destination is Miami is because my owner in San Diego sold me to a brothel in Miami. I was given a train ticket from San Diego to Miami but no money. That is why I don't have a budget for food. The house in Miami is operated by a Jew gangster. He will probably want to break me in the right away, like with laudanum and force. I heard talk. Forcing twenty lays a day, seven days a week, just to break me in. I'll put up with it for a little while, but as soon as I can get my hands on enough laudanum, I'll overdose and escape for good. I will probably be thrown out onto a garbage heap because to them, I am just a piece of meat and spoiled meat at that."

He held her even closer and said, "I believe, I may have an alternative approach. How much were you sold for and how much did you owe to San Diego?"

She leaned back, taking his hands, and said, "I was sold for $200, and I owed $100 to Ed in San Diego, but the houses were being closed down in San Diego. I never would have been able to pay it off on the street."

Jack looked at his fingernails, made a fist, and said, "I have people that would go to five hundred, and they will send someone to negotiate, making sure that, that is the end of it. It's all part of the plan. My pal Nick will take my plan and run with it." He smiled down at her.

She pulled on his T-shirt and said, "I think I better rinse my snot out of it before it dries." She pulled it over his head. Then she stepped back, cocked her head to one side, and said, "I would like to have that washboard belly."

She rinsed the tee out quickly and hung it on one of the towel racks and said, "Let's hope it will dry before lunch."

He went to his suitcase and pulled out another tee, saying, "Why wait?"

She put her hand on his hand that held the new tee and wrapped her arm around his tummy from behind, saying, "Why don't you lie on the bed, and let me take over?"

She reached and snatched his shirt, her dress, and brassier, and moved them to a nearby chair. He sat on the bed. She pushed him, and he fell back, slipping her half-slip to the floor and kicking it toward the chair.

She rolled over on top of him, saying, "How about that? Do you feel me now?"

He threw his arms around her and said, "I want a kiss too—a long kiss and a cuddle."

They broke it up just before lunch. They dressed, and he led her to the club car and had salmon, asparagus, and pilaf. They shared a strawberry float.

She reached across the table, slipping her fingers into his palm, and asked, "May I have a black coffee, hot? I've never had it really black before."

He called the waiter, "Two black coffees." It was as though it had been perking all morning just for her.

She blew across her coffee and asked, "How many white shirts do you have in that little closet?"

"I guess there are six." He sipped his coffee. "Why?"

She looked away. "I thought I might like to wear one in the cabin. I think it might be comfortable"

He sipped his coffee. "Fine with me. What will you do with your dress?"

"I'll hang it that will be good for it," she whispered. "Would you mind terribly if I wash my panties in the little sink?"

He leaned back and asked, "What will you have on while you are washing, rinsing, and drying them?"

With an attempt to appear coy, she tilted her head forward and asked, "Should I wear nothing, or may I borrow a pair of your boxers?"

Leaning forward, he whispered, "Darling, that is entirely up to you."

She raised her eyebrows and said, "Let's get back to the cabin. Do you realize what you did? You called me darling. I want to capitalize on that."

She pulled him all the way to the cabin. Once in the cabin, he slipped his jacket off and pulled his tie until he could slip it over his head and hung them in the closet. He handed her a hanger, and she started unbuttoning from the bottom, and he soon realized she was wearing nothing underneath. She hung the slip in front of the dress, and both were hung outside the closet door. She began unbuttoning his shirt.

"What are you doing?"

She pulled the shirttail out and said, "I want that shirt." She pulled out his T-shirt over his head and said, "I want this shirt." She had him sit on the love seat and began untying his shoes, slipped them off, and pushed them under the love seat. She had him stand, and she unbuckled his belt, and his trousers came down. He kicked them away. The only fabric between them was his boxers. She gave a little tug, and he sat down.

She got up and sat on his lap, saying, "I promise I won't leak."

He said, "How sweet it is." They took solace and succor in each other.

She pulled his face to her bosom and said, "I'll bet your legs are going to sleep."

"Maybe just a little," he admitted.

"I may be leaking just a little." She chortled.

"I'll get you a white shirt and a pair of boxers," he quipped.

She got up and went to wash her undergarments that were soaking in the little sink. After washing, she rinsed and hang them up to dry. She dried her hands and laid the towel on the counter. She turned to see him with outstretched hands holding the white shirt and the boxers.

She took the boxers but refused the shirt, saying, "Sweetie, it is so hot in here, and we could go without our tops. In fact, you could lock the door, and we'll just sit in our boxers and talk until dinner."

He hung the shirt over the back of the chair and locked the door. He turned around, saw her slipping on his boxers, and quipped, "You don't look like a hundred thirty pounds." He drew up in front of her.

She motioned toward the love seat and said, "Sit down, and I'll take your shoes off." He sat and slipped off his T-shirt as well. She pulled off his shoes, stuffing his socks in them, and again, slipped them under the love seat. She looked up at him and asked, "May I wash your feet?"

His retort was "I haven't walked a mile in your shoes yet."

She held her hands out to him and said, "Well, then stand up so I can adjust your pants to get you cool."

He stood with a sigh. He chortled. "How do you propose to cool me with my pants?"

"Just watch." She unbuckled his belt and gave a tug on his pants, but they would not budge.

He said, "I don't feel any cooler."

She tugged even harder, and the trousers came down, but the boxers came down as well.

Looking straight ahead, he gibed, "It is definitely cooler."

She chuckled and smirked. "I just wanted to see all of it." She lifted his boxers up for him to pull up for cover.

He stepped out of his trousers, kicked them aside, and quipped, "I do feel cooler but a little uncomfortable, shy, I suppose."

She took his hand and slowly sat down on the love seat. Looking up, she said, "Will you sit on my right side, with your left arm around my shoulders, and your right hand rubbing my tummy?"

He sat down up against her, put his arm around her shoulders, pulled her to him, and kissed her. Then rubbing her tummy, he said, "Just as you requested."

She laid her head over against his chest and said, "This is my catastrophe."

"I am sorry. I didn't mean to interrupt."

She didn't want to tell the story, but she knew she had to tell it. He wanted to succor her, but he understood that she would have to see it through. She looked out the window with the desert going by and said, "I was born and raised in the valley, went to high school, and graduated. I had dreams of going to college, but my parents could not afford it. I met Bill, my husband, at a high school dance in my senior year. He seemed nice enough, and he always had money. He worked for the granary, in the sales, I guess. I was eighteen when we got married. Family life seemed the way to be. I was pregnant before I was nineteen, and Alice was born the next May, and I was pregnant again before Christmas. Then in September, Barbra was born. And a while later, the arguments started. He wanted a son, and he blamed me for only having girls and not a boy. I had a couple of miscarriages, and he blamed me for that.

"Then, I bore Robert. He was a fat little boy, and I loved him as he came out. Now don't get me wrong. I love my girls too. But a couple of years later, the Depression hit. Bill's hours were cut, and eventually, he lost his job. He started drinking, staying out late at the bars, messing with the barflies. He would come home late, drunk, and beat me. I would hide the kids in the bedroom. I had to stand between him and my kids. He would always want to make up, so he could get to me. I don't remember how many miscarriages I had. He came up with two bottles of Kentucky whiskey. I guess somebody gave it to him. He drank half the first bottle and passed out sitting at the kitchen table. The constable said that the whiskey was mixed with wood alcohol. Poison.

"At the funeral, his parents stole my children. At the trial, the judge said that I was indigent and couldn't care for my children. The verdict was that I was a woman with no means of support, indigent. It was 1930, and everything was closing. The grandparents had a grain farm in the valley. They could feed my children. I was frantic. I didn't know what to do. I found an ad in the LA paper. There was a job at a canning company on the port of San Diego. So I sold what little I had and bought a bus ticket to San Diego. When I got to the canning company, all positions were filled. It just so happened that there were some openings at a new retailer store uptown. I walked all the way uptown, but I was walking to the store, and before the store was a hotel, and there was a hullabaloo, in front of the hotel. Maybe a dozen women were being herded by a bunch of cops, into some kind of wagon. One of the cops grabbed me and shoved me along with those other women into the wagon.

"At the jail, I tried to tell my story, but the sergeant wasn't buying it, and since I had no money for my bail, I spent the night in jail. The next morning, the other women were bailed out, but I was held back. A big fat woman came in and looked at me through the bars. She said, 'I'm boss. I'll pay your bail, and I'll own you. If you run, you will be caught. And you will feel the razor on the souls of your feet. You won't run or even walk for a while, but you will still be on your back, taking them every day, and night.' She held up the bail receipt, saying, 'This is my deed to you. Get in the bus.' I never used my mouth for anything except for eating and talking. They tried to get me to take drugs, telling me that I would feel better or the shame would be easier, but if I took the drugs, the drug would own me, and I would do anything to get that drug."

She broke down and sobbed for a while. He just held her. After a while, he got a wet washcloth and cooled her forehead and her neck. He then leaned her forward, rubbing her back with the cool cloth. She pulled her hair up, and he cooled the back of her neck.

He wrung out the washcloth and quipped, "Tomorrow morning, we will be stopping at Santa Fe, and I will shoot a telegram to my pal, Nick. I am sure this can be handled."

She took his hand and said, "You know, they will try to take me off when we stop in Nashville, Tennessee. And they are big mean guys. I'm scared."

"Nick, has big guys too." He sat down and took her in his arms and said, "They are real mean guys too."

"I can't help it. I'm scared. They want to stick needles in between my toes with laudanum, to make me an addict. They'll inject it in between my toes, so there won't be needle tracks that will be seen by the Johns. I'll be done for."

He held her closer and tighter and said, "We won't let that happen." He held her until twilight.

In the meantime, she fell asleep. When she woke, she looked up at him and smiled. She pulled his head down and kissed him. She moved over to startle him and said, "I want to snuggle and want you to take what you will." She drew his face against her bosoms.

They shared a few moments. A while later, they both realized it wasn't so hot, then they looked out the window at the darkness.

Jack said, "I think it is time to get ready for dinner."

She asked, "Would it be okay if I wore that white shirt?" She pointed to the shirt draped over the chair by the door.

He scowled and said, "The blue dress will be fine."

She made a pouty lip and said, "Let me check my undergarments."

He slipped on his T-shirt. As he was pulling it down, he looked up and saw her drop her boxers, and holding them above her head, she struck a pose.

He said, "My kingdom for a camera."

She tossed the boxers toward the chair. She felt her panties and said, "These are dry, but my brassier is damp, but I think it will be okay."

They finished dressing and headed for the dining car. The host assigned their table, and the waiter led them to a table at the end. He ordered orange roughy and white wine and port for a nightcap.

She closed her eyes and said, "That nightcap made me sleepy."

It was after nine, in that time zone, wherever it was. He let her into the cabin and locked the door behind. He pulled his tie off and hung his jacket in the closet. He looked out the window and said, "It is much cooler on the desert at night." He saw her reflection on the glass.

She burped and asked, "Will you unbutton me?"

He sat her on the love seat, knelt down, and started unbuttoning from the bottom. When he unbuttoned the top button, he pulled the dress away from her shoulders, and having her stand, he slipped the dress away and hung it on the door of the closet.

In the meantime, she slipped off her half-slip. She turned away and asked, "Will you unhook my brassier? I can't reach it right now."

He started to try but stopped, and thinking, he asked, "Do you need to use the latrine?"

She looked around and said, "I gotta pee."

"Is that all?"

"I think so."

He opened the door to the latrine and let her in. She stepped in and started to sit down. He said "Pull your panties down first."

She pulled them to her knees. He kept the door ajar.

She called, "Do you have paper?"

"There are tissues in that tin on the wall."

"What a deal to be rich!" She stepped out, letting her panties drop to the floor and stepping ahead, flipped them up in the air with her toes.

Jack snagged them in midair. He squeezed the crotch and stated, "They are dry as a bone."

She stepped up in front of him and turned with her back to him. Leaning slightly forward, she asked, "Will you now unhook my brassier? I have been fighting this thing ever since and before I went into the latrine."

"Yes, darling, right now, this instant." He fumbled with it a little but finally got it loose.

She pulled it off and threw it on her panties. She walked to the beds, turned, and said, "I can't climb up to that bed. There are no handholds or a ladder."

He stepped over in front of her and feigned to snuggle her bosoms.

She demanded, "Jack, now is not the time."

He snickered, and with both hands at her waist, he lifted her off the floor and sat her on the top bed. He backed up and said, "Girl, you are not hundred thirty pounds. Do you want a sheet or a blanket?"

"I thought I told you. I sleep nude. Covers of any kind keep me awake. Good night."

"Good night."

He brought a pair of silk pajamas, but he didn't want to rummage through his suitcases, so he decided to wear only his boxers. He decided to slip them off and stuff them under his pillow. The nightcap hit him harder than he assumed, and he was out. During the night, Hellen felt such an urge that she needed to visit the latrine again. When she came out, she soon realized that she couldn't get up to the top bed. She knelt down by his head and whispered his name several times, but she could not wake him. So realizing he was sound asleep and noticing that he had the sheet nearly off, she pulled it completely off and rolled in behind him. He was sleeping on his left side, so she pulled her hair up, out of the way. He moved, but he simply laid his arm across her bosom and snorted but did not wake. She slept for a while but woke when another train blew its whistle as the two trains passed. He had not moved.

She laid on her back, thinking, *What would it hurt to feel that washboard tummy, or what I've seen?* She had seen many but not his. *He is so out he'll never know.* She fondled it all so very lightly.

He whispered, "Are you enjoying yourself? I am, but we'll have to get up soon."

She tried to explain.

He said, "Nothing is wrong. You know that I just won't do it."

She tried to make an excuse.

"Be quiet. I didn't say to stop, did I?"

"You mean?"

"That it was nice. And as long as we are friends, we can give comfort."

"You mean, to take all that I can give and give of what you can."

He smiled and said, "It's an old tune, but oh, so true."

She looked down at him and said, "I'm still frightened. Will you hold me for a while?"

"Let's hold each other. I like the way you feel against me."

# THE SETUP

The morning sun gleamed through the window. He held her tight and kissed her like he meant it. He held her tight against himself and said, "You have to do what I am going to tell you. It's important." He bit his thumb and said, "Put your panties on, then go to the latrine, and do what you can do." He took her dress and slip from the hanger and put it as far back on the top bunk as he could. Then he grabbed her shoes and brassier and stowed them at the foot. He was getting dressed when she came out.

She looked around and asked, "Where are my stuff?"

"It's on the top bunk, out of sight. And you will be too as soon as we stop."

She put her hands on her hips, shook her chest, and asked, "Are you going to throw me up there again?"

"Yes, and I'm going to lock you in while I go to the telegraph office. I don't like leaving you alone here, but there is no other choice."

"Hurry back. I'm scared."

The train came to a stop. He took her just above the hips and almost tossed her up on the top bunk; he said, "Now roll over there, and be quiet." He showed her the key. He pushed it up, and it clicked three times. With the key, he locked all three locks. The key went into his pocket, and he locked the door on the way out.

# TELEGRAM

The clerk was the only one at the telegraph office. He took a pad of forms and began to write. The form read as follows:

> To Nick Biltmore.
>
> Urgent need, crew to party to Oklahoma City Day after tomorrow. Bring feminine garment bag, size-8 shoes (5). Need strong arm. Answer now, please.
>
> Jack BMW.

Jack said, "I will wait for a reply."

The clerk said, "This will take some time."

The telegraph began ticking.

"That is him right now."

The clerk sat down, clicked out, send again. The telegraph responded.

Jack said, "Read it off to me."

The clerk read, "All requests affirmed. Have a nice party."

"Give me all the paper copies." He laid a five-dollar bill on the counter. He struck a match as he walked away and lit the two pieces of paper. He checked; there were no carbons. He climbed up the steps to the sleeper car. First, checking for marks, of jimmying; there were none. Unlocking and opening the door, he peered inside. Noticing that everything was just as he left it, he locked the door and went to the top bunk and began unlocking the locks on each clamp. Then he began pulling and unhooking each clamp, all the while whispering, "Stay quiet." He held the bed in place and began to lower it slowly. He didn't want to jostle her.

She soon came into view. Her skin looked somewhat shiny from the sweat. She leaned up on her elbow and said, "It got so hot up here. I thought I was going to croak."

He helped her down from the bed and began wiping her down with a small towel from the vanity. Then he began fanning her with that towel. She grabbed the towel, and they had a slight tug-of-war.

She let go of the towel and asked, "Can I have a wet washcloth?"

"Coming right up." He chortled. He soaked a washcloth and wrung it out but kept it damp.

She turned and beckoned. "Will you cool my back?"

He complied. He soaked the cloth in cooler water and wrung it out again.

She turned back to face him and said, "Would you do my front?"

He tried to appear coy, with a little smile, and yielded again, but when she asked concerning her legs and crotch, he soaked the washcloth in cooler water and wrung it out again. But this time, he held the wet cloth out to her and said, "You're on your own."

She sheepishly took the cloth and began cooling herself. She realized why he did not obey, and she began to snicker and said, "You're afraid of it, aren't you?"

He pushed the buzzer for the attendant and asked, "Are you finished?"

"Yeah, I am just going to soak these panties again." She drew the water and put them in.

He hung his jacket and said, "I think you should go to the latrine."

"Why? I don't need to go."

"Because I have called for the attendant, and you are naked."

"Okay, just knock on the door when it is safe."

Ten seconds later, there was a *tap, tap* on the door. Jack pulled the latch and opened the door.

The waiter said, "May I take your order, sir?"

"Yes, I would like ten roast-beef sandwiches, with mustard on rye, iceberg lettuce, and some big pickles. Also get us a pitcher of gin and tonic with quinine, some lime slices, and a pitcher of ice water with lemon slices, and a bucket of ice."

The waiter asked, "Are you expecting guests, sir?"

"Yes, I think so. Oh! I almost forgot. I'll need a large Sheff's salad. Maybe you will have to get help."

The waiter left. Jack tapped on the latrine door.

Hellen pulled the door ajar and said, "I've been sitting so long on this toilet that now I got to poop. Is there more tissue out there somewhere?"

He began franticly searching for more tissue. He found a whole package on the shelf in the closet. He pushed the door ajar and handed the package to her. He heard the door bell, so he pulled the latrine door shut, saying, "Don't say or do anything until I knock on the door again." He pulled the latch and opened the door to see three waiters.

They were pushing two carts and carrying a large tray. They had everything set up in a matter of seconds. He gave each one a healthy tip, as they each stepped out into the hall. He pulled the door closed and dropped the latch. He knocked on the door, then he heard the toilet flush. She stepped out of the latrine, pulling the door closed behind her. She saw the carts and tray with all the accoutrements.

She looked at Jack and said, "Isn't it nice to be rich and have soft tissue for my bottom and a ton of food to fill me back up again?" She stepped over to the sink and washed her hands. Drying her hands, she said, "Where do we start?"

"First, get those boxers on."

She slipped them on and sat at the little table. He dressed down but kept his boxers. They ate the sandwiches and shared the salad.

She sat back and said, "I would like a big glass of that ice water."

He poured her one, and she took a big draw and held the glass to her forehead and rolled it on her bosoms. She shivered. He snickered.

She sat the glass on the table and said, "This salad is so good, and it is so big. I'll bet it will last until we get to Oklahoma City."

There was a lot leftover when they finished eating. There were covers for everything. He poured a gin and tonic, and they shared it.

She said, "It looks like water. But it tastes better."

"Be careful. It'll sneak up on you." He sat and looked at her.

She ogled him and said, "What?"

"I was just looking at you."

"What could you see in me? I am a piece of excrement, and I belong to a man in Miami, and I am scared to death."

"Tomorrow's another day, and one more day closer to Oklahoma City."

She took a sip of the gin and tonic and asked, "What is happening at Oklahoma City?" She handed him the glass.

He took the glass and spoke over it. "We will be joined by the crew, and the train will not stop, until Oklahoma City."

She shuffled in her chair and asked, "Why did you pick me up at our first breakfast?"

"I simply wanted conversation and perhaps a chess opponent. But when you wiped off your lipstick and made it my choice whether you should reapply it or not, you piqued my interest."

"But remember, you said it was up to me. Did you think I wanted something?"

"I wasn't sure how you were yet, but I learned a little about you when we got to my cabin. You looked around in amazement. But the turning point was when you told me about your painful, smelly feet. I felt such empathy for you that I had to humble myself and wash your feet."

She sat the glass on the table, pushing it back. His hands and forearms lay on the table. She took his right hand in her hands, and looking down at their hands, she spoke. "I have never received such kindness before. Every time I think of it, I have to weep. I can't help it. It just comes, and I don't care to stop it."

He squeezed her hand tenderly and asked, "Do you remember asking me if you could wash my feet? And what was my response?"

She looked straight into his eyes, hesitated, then looked up, paused again, then said, "Not until you have walked in my shoes."

"Close. Not until I have walked a mile in your shoes. But do you know why?"

"I think I know why, but it's hard for me to say."

He looked at the floor that the table leg rested on and spoke. "I have been able to earn several degrees. I have never bore babies or had to protect them. I have never been beaten. I have never lost a spouse, no matter how vile. I have never had my children taken away. I have never been arrested and thrown in jail, without cause. I have never been raped or bought and sold. That is the reason I have empathy for you. My heart aches for you, and we are going to fix some things."

She wiped her eyes, and with both hands, she held both sides of her head at her temples. She sniffed, wiped her nose, and chortled. "It seems that I didn't exist."

He tugged his ear lobe and said, "Hellen is going to vanish."

"How can you do that?"

He shrugged his shoulders, lifted his eyebrows, and quipped, "Your information will disappear. Your arrest in San Diego will be expunged."

Blinking, she asked, "But what about the Jew gangster?"

"He will be dealt with."

She looked out the window, seeing the yellow grainfields in the distance. She seemed to be thinking or dreaming of something secret. He didn't ask. He let her go. He got up and went to the love seat. He decided he wanted a small glass of ice water before sitting down. As he sat down balancing the glass of ice water above his knee, he took a drink, swirling the ice cubes in the water. It made a tinkling sound. He stopped it with his finger and looked to Hellen, hoping not to disturb her dream. He watched her and began to dream himself. There was a knock on the door. They both arose from their dream. Hellen made a dash for the latrine and looked to be sure all was clear. He pulled the latch and pulled the door ajar.

Looking through the crack of the ajar door, he saw the waiter. Jack said, "What is it?"

The waiter asked, "Will you still need both carts? Will it be possible for us to move whatever is left into a single cart? The porter would like to have another cart for the diner."

Jack asked, "May I have some more ice water with lemon slices and another ice bucket?"

The waiter asked, "Would you like me to take the pitcher and the bucket?"

"That will be great. Thank you." Jack held the door open as the waiter pushed the empty cart out.

The waiter said, "I'll be back in two minutes."

Jack asked, "Darling, can you hang for another three minutes?"

She pulled the door open a crack and chortled. "It's okay, I got to pee again anyway."

A little later, the waiter showed up with the ice water with lemon slices and the ice bucket. Jack tapped on the latrine door.

Hellen asked, "Is the coast clear?"

"Yeah, we're all set. Wash your hands, and we'll have dinner."

She dried her hands and laid the towel across her lap and asked, "Have we talked into the night?"

"We still have plenty of time, but I have more to tell you."

She stood and held the towel, folding it, then laying it on the love seat. She sat on the towel. He brought the tray and stood it between them. It held the remaining salad, which was remarkably fresh and quite crisp. There was only one fork. She looked at Jack and showed him a pouty lip.

He shrugged and said, "At the time, I dared only to ask for one fork."

She gave a knowing smile and bit her sandwich. He poked an olive with the fork and handed it to her fork and all. She took the fork and dug into the salad. Of course, they shared. They finished dinner and covered the leftovers and poured refreshments. She took the drink, set it aside, and sat down, pulling him down beside her, but then she rose to her knees, raising her right knee up and over his lap and straddling him.

She leaned back a little and asked, "Do you think they are sagging?"

He pursed his lips and said, "Not that I can see." He let her have her way for a little while. But soon enough, he said, "You need to know what I have to tell you."

"Okay, sweetheart, I am listening." She crawled off and sat on her towel.

He turned to her and asked, "Why are you sitting on your towel?"

"You know why, silly. You got me. We got me warmed up. But I'm not taking any chances on this couch."

He looked at her and grimaced and asked, "What are you talking about?"

"*Wow!* Don't you know what you do to me? Don't you rub my arm or touch my knee. If you do, here it comes."

He looked up, maybe thinking, and said, "Maybe we should stay apart."

"You don't know anything about women, do you, Jack?"

"I guess not."

"Okay, sweetheart. Here are the basics with you and me right now. Don't you dare try to avoid me. I want as much of you as I can get. When you went to the telegraph office, I missed you so much. I was heart sick without you."

"Really, but you were so miserable sweating in the hiding place."

"The worst part was that I was missing you. And when you returned, I wanted to smother you with kisses and take you to my breasts, but I was so hot and sweaty."

"If I had known, I would have taken you in my arms and kissed every drop of sweat."

"You cooled me, and you did the best you could. So I will look for a man that makes me feel as you do. I know what to look for now. Kindness."

"Not just kindness but also empathy and truth."

"I need reassurance. I am still so afraid."

"Don't worry. When you see what we have in store for you, you will not need to fear, ever again."

"Like what? It is just you and me. Who will protect us? I think they will hurt me if they get to me."

"I will not let them get to you. I was the heavyweight boxing champ at UCLA, four years running, and I am a martial-arts expert. And I have a set of brass knuckles stuffed in between the mattress and sideboard. Plus, this train will not stop until we reach Oklahoma City. No one gets on board until then."

"That means, we have tonight and tomorrow to be together as we please?"

"Yes, but when we pull into Oklahoma City, things will change. Several big men will board, and Molly will bring you two garment bags with undergarments and shoes, nylons, and garter belts. Your information will be changed, and your name will be Michelle Ann Biltmore, and that will appear on your California driver's license. The ticket that was bought for you in San Diego will be terminated, and your new ticket will read, 'From Oakland California to Port of Charleston, Carolina.' Your transcripts are on file at the office of admissions at Stanford University, California. You're on your way, lady."

"So before Oklahoma City, I have you all to myself. It's getting hot again. I want you down to your boxers. I don't think I can make it without you."

"I will always be with you. Remember my creed—I believe."

"Believe in what?"

"I'll finish it tomorrow."

She stood by the love seat and said, "Come sit here."

She motioned toward the love seat. He yielded and sat down. She pushed his knees way apart, turned, and sat with her rump against his crotch. Leaning back against his chest, she took both his hands and began to press them against her breasts.

He leaned over her shoulder and asked, "What are you doing?"

"I want you to press my breasts. You can titillate if you wish."

"How long do you want this to go on? And are you sitting on your towel?"

She jumped up, turned around, and scowled at him. He just smiled. She seized the closest towel, folded it, and held it to her rump. She sat back down in place. Once settled, she rearranged his hands to suit herself.

He blew her hair out of his mouth and said, "Is that it? No, thank you for averting a mess on the love seat?"

She looked over her shoulder and said," I'm sorry, darling. Sometimes I forget myself." He scooted forward a little, and she asked, "Are you kicking me off?"

"Don't you think it is time for bed?"

"I guess." She stood and snatched her towel. "I'm going to need this. No pretenses, this time."

Leaving it folded, she spread it where she would be lying against the wall. She crawled in and laid down. Jack turned the lights down and slipped in next to her. His right arm lay across her breasts.

She asked, "Can I have a good-night kiss?"

Saying nothing, he rose by his elbow, bent down, and kissed her as he meant it. He lay back with his arm across her bosoms to sleep. She reached for the end of the towel, gathering it to form a hand-hold, as it were, and pulled it from between her legs, lapping it under her buttocks and over her vulva. She mused and began to dream. He lay motionless all night.

The next day was nearly a carbon copy into and through the night.

# ARRIVING IN OKLAHOMA CITY

It was cool at 7:00 AM. But she was lying on him. She began kissing his face.

He blinked, and she said "Darling, this is absolutely our last morning to wake together, like this. Hold me as long as we dare. I love the way you feel in the cool morning."

"Soon, we will be relegated to wearing suits, ties, and cummerbunds. You will be decked out in silks and satins, garter belts, and nylons. Will you be able to cope?"

"Perhaps it would be better than being on my back and rented to a slob who is half drunk, smelling of cigars and sweat. I think I can cope."

"Darling, do you remember that I told you of my creed? I believe. That is why I am what I am. Remember to look for truth. The past is not even a memory. You are going to start a new life. Live it to the full."

Eventually the train began to slow and finally came to an easy stop. They looked out the window and saw several men in black overcoats and black Stetson hats, a very tall woman, followed by two large men carrying long garment bags, and a man with a trunk on a cart.

He began to get dressed and said, "I think you should get your blue dress on because I believe they will take you down the hall. Don't worry. I will be right behind you."

She slipped on the blue dress but left the undergarments behind. She sat down and slipped on her old shoes that hurt and still smelled. There was a tap on the door; she stood up. Jack opened the door, and there stood Molly and two very large men standing at her side.

Molly stepped in and said, "I believe introductions are in order. You are Michelle Ann Biltmore. And you are Jack. I am Molly, and these nice gentlemen are your bodyguards. If you need something, just call Bill, and either one will answer. I have here your new purse. It contains all your information. You are no longer Hellen, but from now on, you are Michelle Ann."

Michelle said, "I don't even want that purse to touch this filthy dress. It might contaminate it."

Molly squinted, held up a long black trench coat, and said, "Then come out of it."

Michelle pulled the shoulders away and let the blue dress fall to the floor.

Molly handed the coat to her and said, "Let's get rid of those terrible shoes as well."

Michelle stepped out of the shoes and kicked them aside.

Jack looked at her bare feet and quipped, "That hallway floor is kind of rough. Perhaps a pair of my socks might be called for, just for the trip down the hallway." From his garment bag, he produced a pair of black socks. Tossing them to Michelle, he said, "These might suffice."

She sat and slipped the socks on. Standing up, she said, "Maybe they are not fashionable, but they are comfortable."

Molly pushed the door open and said, "Let's get you down the hall to your new room." She turned to one of the Bills and said, "Dispose of that trash on the floor."

Jack asked, "Will you have her ready for breakfast? It'll be a little after ten."

Molly lifted her hands and said, "I'll just have her shower and dress. We're looking at nine thirty. Come for her at ten."

Jack went for her at five to ten. As he approached, one of the Bills, pulled the door open. Michelle stepped out in full dress and a floppy hat. Jack stood back to get a good look, and Michelle hiked her dress up to her knee and displayed real nylons.

She said, "You know, I am wearing a pretty garter belt too. I'd like to show you, but it wouldn't be proper out here in the hall."

Molly stuck her head out and said, "You Bills go with them but don't crowd them."

Michelle took his hand, and as they walked, she said, "Molly fit me with a pad, so I wouldn't have any accidents. She said I am enamored with you. I think it means 'I like or love you too much.'"

Looking at her, he said, "Something like that."

She wanted to swing and dance while holding his hand as they walked along, but she bridled herself. He smiled.

One Bill took the lead; the other brought up the rear. A waiter was asked to have the couple seated and waited at the far side of the table. He motioned for Michelle to be seated in the far seat. Jack took her right hand to assist in her seating. But he lifted her hand to his cheek, and with a slight turn of his head, he kissed her hand with obvious intent. She blushed exceedingly.

Jack took his seat and asked, "Shall I order?"

Michelle, putting her napkin over her mouth, said, "Do you know about my new diet?"

He smiled knowingly. "Eggs Benedict and a fruit bowl with black coffee after."

With the napkin still up to her mouth, she spoke under her breath. "It's a good thing Molly put that pad because, when you kissed my hand, my heart began racing so. Well, I think I'm gushing now. How do you do that to me?"

They finished their breakfast, then sat, sipped their coffee, and whispered many things to each other.

Most of the rest of her meals were taken with Molly. She wanted to verse her in etiquette and proper actions of an educated woman. During their last couple of days on that train, they began seeing less and less of each other. Jack knew it was best for Michelle. There was a stop in Nashville, Tennessee, but there were no gangster types.

The train was parked for fifteen minutes and then on to the port of Charleston. That would be the end of the line for them. Michelle Ann would catch a train for New York City, and he would board a ship for Europe. He would kiss her for what he thought would be for the last time. On that day, he told her that his belief is into Jesus Christ—always truth.

# THE CRUISE

He had two trunks and a couple of suitcases. He carried his suitcases, but the trunks were loaded by the staff. Walking up the gangplank, he was already homesick, or was it seasick? He began sitting up his cabin but waited until they shoved off to go on deck. Coming out of Charleston, the skies were clear, and the sun was hot. He laid on a deck chair, with a small table at his side in easy reach, because there was a large pitcher of gin and tonic and two glasses very close, just in case. He was reading *For Whom the Bell Tolls*. It hadn't become racy or even vulgar yet, just a lot of mountains, rocky trails, and some kind of war.

He heard his name being called. "Jack! Jack!" It was Nick.

He said, "Jack, I have scoured this ship from stem to stern. Is that other glass for me?"

"Sure, help yourself. When did you come on board?"

"My connecting train was late. I got here just in time to pull up the gangplank. I've been searching for you ever since I got on board."

"I've been getting my cabin ready. This is the first day I've been out."

"What are you getting ready for? There are none of feminine persuasion in view, so far."

"I wanted you to meet Michelle. What a woman! She's older, but what the heck."

"Did you try it on for size?" He poured a gin and tonic.

"You know it wasn't like that, but she turned out to be a knockout. She's going to be something. Let's just drink our gin and tonic. Did you recommend this book to me?"

"Of course not, look how thick that thing is. I get stuck on the *Wallstreet Journal*. A real knockout, huh?"

"Yeah, and she was looking at forty but wowee."

"We might meet the author when we get to Paris. You never can tell."

"Say, did you have breakfast this morning? I had a huge one. That is why I got this pitcher of gin and tonic."

"No, I got up too late."

"You better get a big old sandwich with lots of olive oil and a big pickle."

"Yeah, I'll go to the restaurant. See you later."

"Bye, see yah."

He hadn't finished the book, and it was almost a week later, but he was using the same ploy—a pitcher of gin and tonic on the table next to his deck chair, two glasses, and the book on the table. He gave up on finishing it. A woman strolled by. Noticing the book, she stopped and turned back, asking, "How is it turning out?"

He avoided answering, but she persisted and finally asked, "Why are there two glasses? Are you expecting someone?"

He shrugged and said, "Perhaps, you never can tell. Would you care to share some?"

Without asking the ingredients, she accepted and asked, "May I sit down?"

He poured another glass and said, "My name is Jack. May I ask yours?"

"Yes, I'm Tilly, short for Matilda. This is gin and tonic, isn't it?"

Taking in her garb, he said, "Yes, but I insist on quinine."

She wore very loose white shorts, a white cotton blouse, unbuttoned and tied at the waist, no brassier, of course. She also had leather sandals and a floppy straw hat and wire-rimmed sunglasses on. She must be twenty-two or more.

He took a sip and asked, "Are you on vacation?"

She took a gulp and said, "Kind of. I've never been on a boat before."

He took a sip and asked, "Are you with your family?"

She swilled the rest of her drink and asked, "Can I have some more?"

He dropped in some fresh ice cubes in her glass and poured the elixir over. "How are you traveling?"

She had taken off her hat and put it on the small table, pushed the sunglasses back on her hair. "I'm alone. My father is sending me to Germany."

She was very blond, light-skinned with few eyelashes but bright-blue eyes. Her blouse was sleeveless, and he knew she was going to burn. She was a little overweight, and her thighs were pudgy, almost flaccid. He kept mum about it.

He gazed away at the horizon. "Will you study in Germany?"

"Golly, no. I barely got through the eighth grade. But I can read, and I can add, subtract, and multiply, but not divide. That is too hard."

He dropped a couple of ice cubes in his drink. "What are you doing for entertainment on this long ocean voyage?"

It appeared that she thought for a moment. "I'm not sure. I think I'll take what comes."

"How about reading a book or a game of chess?"

"Can I have some ice cubes in my drink? I don't know how to play chess. I have some dime-romance novels in my little cabin, but they never say what really happens."

He dropped a couple of ice cubes in her drink. "What do you think really happens?"

"I don't know. What does he do to get her to a feeling that she wants him so much that she can't resist, and when he gives it to her, she pulls him in, and then everything falls apart after?" She looked past him with empty eyes.

As she stared away for a minute or two, he thought, *She must be out of tears.* But he didn't know how to help. He looked to the stern and saw the clouds, gathering in the West.

It was not a threatening storm; it was in the past. "Why are you going to Germany?"

She stared at him with her mouth agape. "I'm going to Hamburg."

He then knew why. He had read reports out of Hamburg Institute. They were using poison to terminate pregnancies. It was inhumane and, in some cases, lethal. He looked at her and thought, *Such a waste.*

He looked her up and down. "You have some thinking to do. You can have that baby, put it up for adoption, or keep it and raise it on your own or go on to Hamburg and flush it. The procedure may kill you or make you sterile. It is all up to you."

She turned to him. "Do you think I can find a man who can love me after all this? I mean, if I keep the child or put it up for adoption, will someone still love me?"

He put both his hands on both her knees, looked into her big blue eyes, and said, "There are millions of people in this world, and tomorrow is another day. Think of how precious life is."

Pushing her glass away, she replied, "I better not have that anymore. I'm getting off at London, and I'm going to have this baby and raise it on my own if I must."

He handed her hat to her. "Search out a man that's worthy of you."

They hugged and shared a kiss. From then until she got off at London, each time they met on board, they hugged and shared a kiss even as she began showing. Jack and Nick caught up with her a couple of days before arrival.

Nick acted as their spokesperson. He said, "I know this wonderful family who would be pleased to care for you through your trials. We have already telegraphed them, and they will be expecting you."

Jack handed her the name and address of that family. She thanked them both, sealing it with a hug and kiss for the both of them. Nothing more said, but they would both be benefactors for her until she was found by someone to love her.

They were docking at London, and he still had not finished that book.

Going down the gangplank, Nick called back to Jack, "Let's not wait on this ship for three days. Let's get a boat for Dunkerque this morning. We'll just have our luggage sent over."

"Sounds like a splendid plan, and you'll handle the paperwork," Jack quipped.

"Just in your way, Jack. :eave me with the heavy lifting."

They stood on deck, leaning over the railing. Nick stood up. "Say, Jack, why didn't you pick up another woman after you saved Tilly's baby?"

"That just made me think about what is important in life. And I thought about something that Michelle Ann said to me." He stood up and turned to Nick.

The boat rocked a little. Nick grasped the railing. "Well, don't keep me in suspense. What did she say?"

"She said that she wanted to take me to her breast. What does that mean?"

"I heard that she is enamored with you. Maybe that fits in there somehow. Let it all go. Let's enjoy France." Nick put his arm around his shoulder. "Just lighten up, and don't be so serious. Let's have some fun."

They looked over the railing at the swirling water. The docks came into sight and the jostling of the actual docking and finally standing on dry ground.

Jack said, "Let's set up a base in Rouen. Look for a flat."

"Good thinking. That way, we can travel where we wish," quipped Nick. "There is the bus for Rouen. It's loading right now."

Jack called, "Let's hurry."

# FRANCE

They were able to catch the bus and got two seats next to each other. They began to practice their French.

A woman sitting across from Nick said, "Your accent is strange."

"How so?" quipped Jack.

She chortled. "Your consonants are not hard enough."

"But how do I do it?" quipped Nick.

She gave him some examples. She seemed quite taken with him. She was somewhat skinny. Her face was careworn and drawn. She asked Nick where he was staying in Rouen, but he had to tell her that they hadn't found a flat. She offered to help find accommodations.

Jack, looking at her hands, saw that they were smooth and fine and said, "I wouldn't mind trading places with you so that you and Nick can become better acquainted." And so it went.

As they departed the bus, Nick asked, "Why don't we find a sidewalk café, eat, and discuss our plans? By the way, Jack, this is Erma. She is really helping me with my French."

"Are you hungry, Erma?" Jack quipped.

"Yes, I'm quite famished. I haven't had breakfast, and it is nearly lunchtime." Erma chortled.

They found the corner café, took a table, and sat near the street. A waiter took their order and withdrew. Erma began to admonish them that they should not get their residences even in the same buildings.

She asked, "What if one of you has a guest that the other might recognize or a guest of one might recognize the guest of the other? Keep it friendly."

"That sounds plausible," agreed Jack.

"Let me propose this. I'll show Nick around, and I'll call a friend of mine to assist Jack. How does that sound?"

"Okay, let's eat." Nick chortled.

They finished lunch, and Erma suggested a bar just around the corner. They ordered anisette, and Erma went to the phone and quickly returned. She stepped up next to their table, took her drink in hand, and downed it in one swallow.

Backing up a step, she said, "Mal, will be here momentarily. You should set her up a drink." Erma downed another anisette, took Nick by the arm, and virtually dragged him out of his chair, saying, "We're going to my place. Mal will take good care of you."

Jack paid for Mal's drink and sat it on the table. Two minutes later, Mal strolled in. She sported a white sleeveless cotton blouse and a tight gaberdine skirt, cut just below the knee, with no nylons.

She stepped forward. "Are you Jack?"

"I am if you're Mal," Jack quipped.

She looked at the drink on the table.

"Sit down. I'll tell you what I want," quipped Jack.

She hiked her skirt above her knee and sat. "Is this drink for me?"

"Go ahead. I'd like a flat here in Rouen. I plan to travel, and I will use this as my base. Money doesn't matter."

She swallowed the anisette in one slug, pulled a comb from her hair, and let it fall. It was blond and heavy. "Is that all you're looking for?"

He downed his drink in a single swallow and looked at the glass. "You never know what might come up."

"My friend said that you and your friend are both single, but she wants you in separate buildings. Is there a problem between you two?"

"No, she is just trying to protect our privacy." His attention turned to her lips. They were quite smooth and supple-looking. "Would you care for another drink?"

She held up her glass and looked through. "Yes, thank you. Where would you care to visit?"

"Paris, of course, Lyon, Montpellier, Cannes, and Nice. Would you have any suggestions?"

She took a sip of her new drink. "Paris is mostly a show town. Lyon and Montpellier will have different customs, but Nice has gambling. Both Nice and Cannes have nude beaches for sluts."

He leaned in supporting himself by his elbows, peering into her hazel eyes. "I might enjoy the shows. I like to learn new customs, and I might gamble a little, but nude beaches—that wouldn't affect me. You see, I sleep nude, and may not dress until eleven."

She sat back and took his measure. "Would you mind terribly if I have another?"

"Not at all. Let's make it a double." He stepped to the bar and ordered the drinks.

While waiting for the drinks, he turned to see her applying lipstick and rouge. He turned back quickly to pick up the drinks. Stepping back to the table, he set the drinks on the table and took his seat.

She looked at his hands on the table. "What are you thinking?"

He looked at his fingernails. "I don't think you want to know right now."

"Would it shock me?"

"I doubt it. What do you do here? Are you a rental agent?"

"Okay, here is how it works. If I show you a flat and you take it, I earn a commission. However, let's say you want to go to Lyon, and you need an escort, I might volunteer, but if not, I have a regular job at a bar. I'll give you my number, just in case."

"Does Erma work the same way?"

"Basically, yes, but I think she likes Nick. Don't tell on me."

"And you don't like me?"

"I do, but I am not supposed to. Don't tell on me. In fact, I would like to go to Cannes with you."

"Let's go look at some flats."

"We'll catch the bus."

"No, I want to get a cab."

"Okay, it's your money."

"Here is a trick used in the US. Pull your skirt above your knee and stick your ankle out."

As soon as she did that. There were brakes squealing, and a cab stopped right in front of her. They got in, and Mal told the cabbie the address, and they were off. The cab stopped in front of a three-story building. They got out, but Jack gave the cabbie two francs, which was short, and told him to wait. Mal rang the buzzer, and the front door opened, and they walked down a hallway, but just inside, there was an office with a counter and a window opening to the hall. They went up a stairway, two flights. Mal took a few steps down a hallway, and looking up at the number on the door, she pushed it open and stepped in. Jack fallowed.

Taking a few steps into what appeared to be living room, Mal said, "This is the first one, sixty francs a month."

Jack walked into another room and stood looking out a window. "I suppose it is furnished?"

"Yes, and you can sign the lease downstairs in the office."

He walked into a bedroom completely furnished. Mal jumped on the bed. "Come, let's try it out." She rolled back and forth a few times. Jack frowned. She sat up immediately.

He stood over her and asked, "Is this the best one you have?"

"Yes, it's the only one left," she whimpered.

He walked into the bath. There was a bathtub, a basin, and a water closet. He retreated to the kitchen. "Can you cook?"

"Of course, I can cook. I am a Frenchwoman."

He went downstairs to the office and signed the lease, got power, and water on. But he was told that the water was not a problem, but the gas would be furnished, but there was no electricity. All the lamps were gas and will be ignited by a flint switch and control. He learned that everything would be on by the evening. He went back upstairs and found Mal lying on the couch in the living room. He took a seat in an overstuffed chair, across from her.

She pushed herself up on one elbow, pulled her skirt up to midthigh, cocked her knee, and asked, "What is on your mind?"

He paused, pulling on his earlobe. "I'm trying to decide what to do until dinner."

"You could visit a park. People do that in the afternoon here." She ran her thumb and finger along the bottom seam of her skirt. "But it is not good alone."

He uncrossed his legs and sat up straight. "Perhaps you might know of a young woman who would like to accompany me?"

She rolled, sitting up. "I might know a girl, but I am available. But if you would prefer a younger one, I can arrange it."

"I thought that you were just here to show me this flat, and that's all."

"Well, yeah, but I don't want to go back to work at the bar, and you're rather cute and all. Besides, you're more interesting."

"What sort of garb would be appropriate for the park?"

Standing up, she said, "First of all, you will have to take off the white shirt. Are you wearing a T-shirt?"

He looked down at his pants. "Yes, but what about my trousers?" He took off both shirts but put the white dress shirt back on. "I'm not used to going without my T-shirt."

"Now let's go to my place. I need to change my togs."

They jumped in the cab and headed to her place, which was an old tenement building. "I'll wait in the cab," demanded Jack.

"Nonsense," quipped Mal, "I have girls I want you to meet."

They went up a single flight of stairs because it was only two stories. Mal crashed through the door into what appeared to be a living room and three bedrooms all in one.

Mal said, "Everybody, this is Jack, and this sitting on the bed is Gigee, and in the toilet is Giselle."

Jack said, "Hello, everybody."

Mal began rummaging through clothes laying on the floor and undressing at the same time. Soon, she was naked except for a pair of panties and stood holding a pair of shorts and a light-colored midriff blouse. She jerked the shorts on and slipped the blouse on as they went out the door. In the cab, she tied the bottom in a not to close it. She pulled her hair out of the back of her blouse and shook it out. She gave the cabbie directions.

She looked at Jack and said, "Don't we make a fine couple?"

"Are we going to sit on benches or what?"

"No, we will lie on the grass."

"Wouldn't a blanket be better?"

"Oh! Look, there is a merchant selling blankets."

The cabbie stopped in front of the stand. Jack jumped out and bought a nice one, then back in and on to the park.

Mal said, "I know a great spot by the water. It is a little secluded but lots of sun."

"Next time, we should bring wine and cheese."

"It's around this next bend. I'll get the blanket. Can you pay the cabbie and send him off?"

"Yeah, I've got it. Go ahead."

She grabbed the blanket and disappeared. As he came around from the other side of the cab, he heard her but couldn't see her until she raised her hand and waved at him. He walked toward her but had to walk around some rushes to get to that spot.

She laid on her side, chewing on a piece of grass. "Come sit and take your shirt off and lie next to me."

He laid on his side facing her, and she was facing him. He rose up supporting himself by his elbow. "Would you mind if I ask you a rather personal question?"

She threw the little grass stem over her shoulder. "No, go ahead and ask. I promise not to be upset."

He pursed his lips and asked, "How old are you?"

Her brown eyes flashed. "I'm twenty-two and fifty-two kilos, and five feet, eight inches. I'm sorry. I promised to not be angry. I just feel like a fish on a hook."

"I'm twenty-six, two hundred twenty pounds, and six feet, five inches. I was just trying to make conversation."

"Lie on your belly."

"Why?"

"I will titillate your back."

She began kissing and giving butterfly kisses. Then she stopped. "Would you mind if I get comfortable?"

As he turned back to leaning on his elbow, he said, "No." But he almost choked on his word because she was not just lying as before, but now she was nude.

She rubbed her foot up on her ankle, almost to her knee. "What do you say about the look of me now?"

"Stunning, absolutely stunning."

"Do you feel uncomfortable with me like this?"

"Not really, I rather enjoy it. Can I ask you some more questions?"

"Yes, of course. May I lean against your tummy?"

"Of course, there is no law about it."

She took his hand and held it up to look at it. "Some say I am a little fat, but I say it is because I'm a little short. Do you think I am just fat or pleasingly plump?" She rested his palm on her breast.

He looked down at the profile of her face. "Definitely plump. What do you think of me?"

"I think you are handsome and rich but also kind. But I don't know if you like me."

"I don't know either. What do you think it would take for you to know that I like you?"

"I think it would be clear if you request more from me."

"What more would I request? What do you want from me?"

"A Frenchman would be all over me already."

"I'm not like that. Where are your parents?"

"My father was a Spaniard. He died for Franco, so my mother said."

"Where is your mother then?"

"She is laying up in the house. She will never come home. This Depression has ruined a lot of lives." He took her in his arms and held her close.

He could feel her jerk with each sob. He held her and let her cry. He knew he would have to let her go sooner or later. He would give her as much as he could as long as he could. She looked up at him with her big brown eyes. It was just miserable. He sat on the blanket with her rump in between his legs close. She leaned back against him, and he wrapped his arms around her belly and bosoms with the white shirt draped over them. He let her whimper and breathe deeply. It was a good long while before she became totally conscious, and he let her rest even more before he let her get dressed.

He got a taxi, took her to her place, but told her not to say anything about what happened, but she had to tell her girlfriends, but he took them all out to dinner, anyway. Gigee, who was seventeen, was letting him practice French; but Giselle, who was nineteen, wanted to make out all the time. They knew that he would travel, and some would be assigned to accompany him. They would all go to Cannes and Nice. They knew how he preferred to sleep.

*****

He met a woman in Lyon of a Jewish family—a pretty young girl just out of grammar school. His mother would have been proud. She had long blond hair, brown eyes, and hips as wide as could be and buxom beyond belief. She wanted to get married right then and get pregnant before they would get on the boat. No, thanks, so back to Rouen he did. The snow came to Europe, but the flat was warm.

Year 1936 finally arrived, and spring was in the air. He sent the girls to Britain one at a time. Mal was the first to go. She didn't want to go, but she heard the Germans were brutal, so she was afraid for her mother, but there was nothing to do. Gigee was ready to head for safety, and Giselle wanted to go with him, but he had to refuse her. They would all be safer in England. They were taken in by families in Liverpool.

He went to Paris and saw a few shows but spent his free time searching for Nick. It was said that he was smitten by Erma and was dallying in Rouen. With the look of her, she surely had some tricks up her sleeve. He sent him a telegram, saying they should meet in Belgium, if it was convenient. Jack was reading about the political event taking place in Germany. So he took a train to Hamburg, out of Paris.

# VILE GERMANY

On the train, to Hamburg, there were three switches. On the first leg of the journey, his fellow travelers were two Frenchwomen and a Basque gentleman, who did not speak any French. The two women and Jack became acquainted quickly. The Basque slept. They were rather thin, but one was from Lyon going to Frankfurt. She had short dark hair and was not wearing a hat. The other was trying to get to Belgium. She wore a flapper style and held her skirt well above her knees, with her legs spread, and she spoke in an enticing manner, almost lustful.

The train stopped, and they departed, but Jack remained and was soon accompanied by a new group. There were two men and one woman. They all spoke German. Now Jack's German was broken, to say the least. The men were chatting among themselves. The woman was thickset, not fat, tall, and a comely face. She sat on her open coat, with her skirt hiked up past her knees, showing her pale white legs, with no stockings. She railed on about their new government. The train stopped again, but no one left or entered the compartment. The woman gathered her coat around herself and leaned against the window, closing her eyes.

All most an hour later, the train stopped, and Jack looked out the window to see the placard on the station that read, "Hamburg."

Jack began to gather his belongings, and stepping through the crowd, he made his way to the steps to exit that car. He stepped onto the platform and headed toward the office, but the Golden family caught him and introduced themselves to him and vice versa. David, the father, put his arm around his shoulders and rushed the whole group off the platform and onto the street, where there were taxies waiting. They all piled into a single cab.

The cabbie said, "I have to charge you extra. This is too much weight for my cab. Something might break."

They arrived at the house. It was dark outside. David, unlocked the front door, and Anna, his wife, ran in and began lighting all the lamps downstairs. David sent all the children upstairs to bed, except for Cathy, his eldest daughter.

He called to Anna, "We will take coffee in the parlor."

Jack asked, "How did you know I was going to arrive tonight?"

David motioned for Jack to take a seat. "I received a telegram that you left Paris on that train. It is the only one out of France. Simple deduction."

Their chairs were adjacent to each other, and Cathy's mother was sitting on the end of a couch with Cathy standing next to her. Cathy and Jack were introduced, and Cathy curtsied. Then the mother took Cathy to fetch coffee for Jack. When they returned, Cathy served Jack his coffee and sat on the floor at his feet. The mother did the same for David, and it was clear that she was definitely pregnant. David sipped his coffee.

"I am sure that Cathy will make you good wife, and if Anna is a foretelling of her fertility, you can have many children. She is fifteen and looking forward to family life."

Jack finished his coffee and set the cup and saucer on the small table next to his chair. "I'm kind of tired after the trip. May I lie on the couch?"

Cathy jumped up and started to carry off his cup and saucer, but mother said, "Did you ask Jack if he was done, or does he want more?"

Cathy whimpered, "I'm sorry. Would you like some more?"

"Anna has the guest room readied for you, with toiletries and towels at your disposal," quipped David.

In the hallway, Cathy asked her mother, "Can I show Jack to his room?"

"Okay, but don't let your father see. It is still improper."

Cathy took Jack's hand. "I'll show you to your room." She pulled him up the stairs and down the hall to the right. She stopped and turned. "It's the door on the left." It was ajar, so she pushed it open and stepped in. Pulling Jack in behind her, she turned and asked, "Are you coming from France?"

"Yeah, I guess."

"Did you have a French girlfriend? Did you French-kiss her?"

"It's not like that over there. What do you want?"

"Can we French-kiss?"

"Right now?"

"I've never done it, and I have heard it is wonderful."

"Really, well, there is a special technique. Here it is. You must fallow my direction. First, we should be in an embrace. Then you should hold and caress the back of my head. Then a light kiss with our mouths a little open, and then my tongue in your mouth, then your tongue in my mouth, but never both at the same time."

She backed up and leaned against the vanity and just stared at him, with her mouth wide open.

He said, "That's too wide." He took her in his arms. "Now wrap your arms around me." He leaned her back and gave her a French kiss, then said, "Now give me your tongue."

When he turned her loose, she gasped, "I want more."

"We will have some time together tomorrow. We will practice some other things."

*****

He had a fitful sleep that night but woke early. He heard David's knock on his door. After dressing, he ambled down the stairs and saw the whole family at breakfast. He stood in the doorway, watching the activity. Cathy went to him and pulled him back out the doorway and pushed him out of sight and began kissing him.

"Come, I'll serve you breakfast." She never sat down; instead, she waited on him hand and foot.

David and Anna smiled at him. The children giggled.

Finishing, David picked up the morning paper and asked Jack, "Do you read German?"

"I struggle at it."

"Well, let's go see what we can get out of this."

They took their seats in the parlor. "Anna, bring us each a coffee."

Cathy came rushing in with a cup and saucer and set a coaster on the tabletop and sat down at Jack's feet. Anna came in with the same articles but went back to the kitchen to finish her work. David smiled. "She is due any minute."

Jack tried to read, but he noticed that Cathy was always looking up to him. Jack gulped his coffee. "I think I would like to take Cathy for a walk."

Immediately, Cathy jumped up and cleared his place and asked, "May I go change my shoes?"

"Yes," quipped Jack.

David smiled.

She ran upstairs and returned with different shoes and a different blouse.

The sun was up, and it was getting warm. They stepped off the front step and down the very short sidewalk to the street.

At the street, he turned and asked, "Where can we go to be alone?"

"Where did you go in France?"

"We could go to a park and lie on the grass but not here. I've seen some thugs around here. I don't trust them around here."

"I've heard that some lovers go to the woods, but I don't think that is safe either. I am getting anxious. I'm going to kiss you right here on the street."

"Does your father ever leave the house?"

"He will go to the shoe shop and haberdashery after eight, and he won't be back before dark."

"Does this house have a back porch? I'll bet there is an old couch or some chairs to sit on. As soon as your father leaves, we'll go check. Do you think your mother will ever go out there?"

"I have never seen her out there. She thinks there are rats."

Jack backed up to a tree on the side of the street and put his hands in his back pockets.

"What are you doing?"

"Come over here and act like we are talking, for when your father comes out."

"Here he comes."

"Is there a back or side door to the house?"

"I think there is a side door, but I don't know where it goes."

"Let's go to the back first."

She twisted the knob and pulled the door open, and they went up two steps, and inside, there were some things covered in dusty sheets.

Jack pulled the sheet back and revealed a comfy couch. Jack stood back and said, "Just for us."

She sat down and pulled him down beside her. "Do you remember how?" Jack quipped.

She fluttered her blouse. "I'm ready right now."

He took her arms and pulled her to him. "When you come on, you come on."

"Well, come on."

He took her in his arms and kissed her long and deep, and when he let her up, she gasped, "Oh, yeah!"

"Give me all of yours," he groaned.

She grasped the back of his head, pulling it to her, kissing him, and he let it in. He felt her hot breath on his cheek. She kept pushing for more and more. He inadvertently brushed against her breasts, and she clinched even tighter to him. She began to pant, then drew up, and began to relax. She opened her eyes and looked up at him, then lay her head on his shoulder.

Pulling in a deep breath, she said, "I want this always."

Staying ahead of her, he asked, "I know why you changed your shoes, but why did you change your blouse?"

She bashfully lowered her head as to hide her timidity and said, "I took off my brassier and put this light silk top on, so I could offer my breasts to you. I want to entice you."

He leaned back to look at her. "Well, let's see."

She gathered the blouse up to just below her neck. "See, I'm a woman fully grown. I thought you might fondle me while we share a long kiss. What do you think?"

He shook his head and smiled. "You don't need to hold your blouse up. I can get under it."

They were entwined a couple of hours that morning. Cathy sat up.

Jack looked at her. "What is it?"

"It's almost lunchtime. Mother will be looking for us," Cathy spouted.

Jack pulled the sheet back over the couch so it looked untouched.

Cathy tried to pull her blouse down tight. "Does it look wrinkled?"

He looked her up and down. "No, you look fine. Silk won't wrinkle at all."

Jack saw the side door; it was a funny setup. As they went out through it, Jack turned to close it; he realized that it was a part of the side paneling.

As they walked along beside the house, Cathy asked, "Was I good at French-kissing?"

Jack looked ahead. "Yes, but that is not the point. Can you—will you love me?"

She just looked up at him as they walked around to the front of the house. Jack knocked on the front door.

Cathy's mother answered the door, "Where have you been? I have been waiting. The soup is hot, but you will need to compete Jack's lunch. I fed the children, but you are expected to wait on Jack. I can't guide you. I will need to lie down. The baby wants to come out now, but if I lie down, it may stop." She turned and went upstairs.

Cathy set his place, then rushed into the kitchen, and brought him a hot bowl of soup. As he began to sip the soup, Cathy disappeared into the kitchen. He was nearly finished when she brought his main course and cleared the soup bowl.

He raised his head. "Aren't you going to eat?"

"I'll eat after I have taken care of you."

He finished his lunch, and she cleared his place and came back to him. "Will you take me into the parlor? Mother is asleep, and the children are down for their naps."

He knew what she had in her mind, but he followed suit. He was aware that they would be absolutely alone, and he was aware that she had changed her blouse again, and this one was a flower print with a button front. She took his hand and led him into the room and closed the door. He gave her leeway to do as she pleased. He decided not to instigate anything. He sat with his hands in his lap.

She squirmed a little. "Wouldn't you like to kiss me?"

He didn't answer but stared her down.

"We are all alone, and you can have your way with me." She chortled.

"So you say. Are you setting a snare for me?" He chortled.

"Oh, on the contrary, I wondered if I have enamored you."

"Not so much as a tiny ember. Come sit on my lap and chance to ignite a tender flame."

"Do you plan to woo me with your spectacular prose alone?"

She leaned away and unbuttoned her blouse and pulled it open. She pulled his head to her and began kissing, her favorite. His right hand found its way under her blouse, and with his left hand, he began lifting her butt with his entire hand. She began kissing him frantically down to his neck.

She gasped and fell back and began trying to catch her breath. Breathing heavily, she said, "I need to rest a moment."

"Are you all right? Perhaps we should slow a little."

She lowered her head, then raised it again, and swallowed to speak. "I don't know what it is or how to explain it, but when you pulled on my butt, something in my lower belly, there was a spasm drawing for something. I felt such a longing, almost a craving. I think

I want something, but I don't know what. I thought I might crawl on top of you and smother you with me."

"*Aha,* that's it! We cannot ever be intimate again unless I come for you in years to come. You may have met someone in the interim. I hope that will be the case." He wanted to take her in his arms and comfort her, but he didn't dare. He pushed her off his lap and sat her at his side. "When will your father have a day off? I need to have a serious discussion with him."

"I don't understand. You make me feel so—I don't know how to express it, but I'm afraid that I'll long for you all the while. Father is home all day, the day after the Sabbath."

He looked at her attire. "You should button your blouse and tuck it in. We must be discreet."

"Shall I make you a coffee?"

"I would enjoy some."

She went to the front door and picked up the newspaper that had been slipped through the mail slot, took it to Jack on her way to the kitchen, and lay it on the table next to him. She was in the kitchen, a mere moment, then appeared, with his coffee. He was reading the paper by the time she returned. She sat his coffee on the table, and she sat down at his feet. Each time, he looked down at her, he would find her looking, longing back up to him.

Days began to vanish into night, and night to dawn, and over and over again until the morning after the Sabbath. At breakfast, he was realizing that her mother no longer guided Cathy's actions because she did everything for Jack, from pouring his coffee to buttering his toast. He drank down his glass of tomato juice and wiped his lips with the napkin on his lap.

Cathy said softly, "May I pour you another serving of tomato juice?"

"No, thank you." He got up to leave the table.

David was making his way into the parlor.

Jack walked rather quickly, hoping to catch him before he would take his seat. "Mr. Golden, can we talk in your study?"

"I suppose." They went into the study.

They were followed by Anna and Cathy, both carrying the coffee for each man. Anna served his coffee to David and departed to the dining room. But Cathy, after serving Jack his coffee, sat down at his feet. Jack leaned forward, laying his hand on Cathy's head.

"I want you to go help your mother. Clear the table in the dining room." Lowering her head sheepishly, she rose and slowly made her way out of the study.

"Are you that concerned?" asked David.

"Terribly. Do you believe this room is secure?"

"I believe so. Let me close the door." He went and closed the door, then returned to his seat behind the desk.

Jack cleared his throat. "Did you hear of the night of the long knives?"

"I read about it in the newspaper, but that was some time ago."

"Yes, 1934, as matter of fact. Do you recall what happened?"

"A few of the Hitler youths or Brownshirts were killed."

"One point three million to be correct, and those that were spared were planted into the regular police. They began rounding up dissidents and Jews and shipping them to concentration camps that were built in secret. And they will come for you and your family. It is only a matter of time."

"But I have papers and passports, and I feel safe with the new administration. I pay my taxes, and I follow the law."

"None of that will save you and your family. They will bang on your door, and when you show them your papers or passports, they will rip them apart and throw them on the floor. Remember, you won't be dealing with kind authorities but vile, evil savages without morals. They may smash your face with a rifle butt, and as you lie on the ground, with you choking on your own blood, you'll see them dragging out your wife and children to who knows where, usually jail. They will be taken away from you, and you can only imagine their fate. Remember, those animals have no morals, only hate for you and your family and all Jews."

"My collogues and I are members of the same clubs, and my family and I have attended many state dinners, and I am sure that such friendships will supersede any political disagreements."

"I suppose you believe that your coercion will take the shape of pleasant dialogue, possibly in a court of law. Mr. Golden, that is not where these savages administer their brand of justice. No, it is in a cold, dark cell, where the cries, begging, and screams cannot be heard. They have no rules of conduct. An adolescent girl would be raped by twelve or thirteen men, one at a time, in succession. As soon as the last one is finished, the first one comes again, all daylong into the night or until she becomes a blithering imbecile. I don't want that for any child or person. A man or boy would be tortured using a pair of pliers, belts, or whips to see what they might disclose before they are shot, burnt, or hanged. I don't take pleasure in this stark warning, but at the think tank at UCLA, we have been keeping a close eye on these monsters. Get out while you can. The time is short, and the gold you have stored in the safety-deposit box will be riffled, and you will lose all. There is only one train allowed to leave Germany bound for Paris a week."

"I don't see how I can give up everything and run."

"There is a time coming when it will be too late. Go to your store and watch all the people being carried away." Jack shrugged and moved to the parlor. He tried to hold a feeling of ambivalence toward Cathy, even though he had empathy for her. He had to save her by convincing her father of the severe cruelty of these monsters. The children were a given. Time went on until the end of the week.

*****

David arrived home early, motioning for Jack to join him. He led him directly to the study, allowed him in, and closed the door behind him. "I saw something despicable today," he growled.

Jack beheld his anger but stayed mum.

David stomped back and forth in front of his desk. "As you suggested, I stood behind the glass window, on my storefront, and watched as a group of thugs dragged Joseph Abrams from his store. He is a brother in my lodge. I could not imagine why he was being arrested. But they forced him to his knees and pulled his coat down to constrain his arms, and then they began striking him about the head. What appeared to be the arresting officer kicked him in the back, and the mob threw him in a wagon of some sort. I could see that there were others in there with him. He fell to the floor as it drove away.

"Later that day, there were other arrests in the same fashion. But later that day, some of my staff said that Abrams had been reported to the authorities as a dissident." David whirled around. "What if I had been reported on? He could not protest at all. They just beat him unconscious and hauled him off. What chance would I have or my wife or my children? I think you are right, Jack. Can you help me? Will you help me?"

"Yes and yes, but we must follow a plan. Do you agree? I was hoping you would see the light. First, do you agree that to leave is the only choice you have?"

"But will I be able to save anything, and once we are out and safe, how can I start again?"

"First, do you ever return any articles to Paris or cities of manufacture?"

"Yes, of course, why?"

"Let's say, you are returning shirts. They must be shipped in boxes. Your Monet would fit into one of those boxes. But one box in a case of twenty-four. Shoes boxes will have false bottoms, but jewels or small pieces of gold will be concealed in the soles, a small trick but highly effective. You must take any gold ingots or gold jewelry from the safe-deposit boxes. They will be broken into and robbed. You must ship everything by freight. Don't even let your wife hide jewelry in her hair. They are wise to check that. Where you have paintings hanging on a wall, the painting will leave a mark. Take them all down and store them in an unused room and have the walls where they were hanging painted over. Two coats. If you are going to put this plan into motion, you must move quickly, but be as inconspicuous as possible. You might send your wife and children on holiday to Paris."

"That is a splendid idea, plus she could meet the freight at its destination."

"Now for you, you should not do anything out of the ordinary. Do everything as you normally would."

By the end of the week, the house was nearly empty.
David said, "It's just a house." It sold to a constable.

*****

Jack was on his way to Amsterdam, but he would cancel. He had not been assigned to meet anyone because many were already evacuating. He had a layover in Berlin to measure the social climate, which turned out to be a firebrand. His first glimpse of revelry was a dance hall with a large band and dancers on platforms on the sides of the hall. They were for the most part nearly naked and undulating robotically. He looked at the people on the large dance floor.

A bawd stepped up next to him and asked, "Will you buy me a drink?"

"What is yours?" Jack chortled.

"Peppermint Schnapps," she snapped.

Jack turned to the bar. "Two Peppermint Schnapps," he called to the bartender.

He laid ten marks on the counter under his hand, holding them until the drinks showed up.

"Bring the drinks to that empty table there," she quipped.

The drinks slid down the bar. He lifted the hand, picked up the drinks, turned, and stepped to the table, setting both drinks on the table, and took a seat. He looked at her hard.

She sipped her drink. "Come closer. You can't touch me from there, or shall I sit on your lap?"

He pushed his chair back. "Come on."

She looked totally surprised but got to her feet, and wrapping her arm around his back, she slid onto his lap. She took his drink from his hand, and raising it to his lips, she forced about half of it down his throat. He nearly choked. She pulled his face to her bosom and began to rub his nose on them. He pushed her away but grabbed her drink and forced her to drink, nearly the whole glass full. She began coughing with her mouth open. He saw that most of her teeth were rotten.

She finally got ahold of herself. "I'm afraid, you might punch me in the mouth."

He pushed her off and made her sit in the chair she came from. "I'll buy you another drink, and then you can go try to find a trick somewhere else."

He left the half-full glass on the table and walked toward the entrance. As he went up a couple of steps, he turned, and looking back, he saw her guzzling the rest of his drink. He stepped out into the frigid night air and walked toward his hotel. He saw a street prostitute on every corner. They each called to him as he passed. They offered a lay for a warm place. He passed them as quickly as he could. As he entered the lobby of his hotel, the night clerk asked if he wanted a courtesan for the night. He didn't answer, just continued upstairs.

*****

He visited several other bars and dance halls but found himself in a reading room and reading the local newspaper. On a bulletin board, he found an advertisement for a room to let, and he inquired. It was two rooms, plus a bath, furnished. The landlord was a woman by the name of Hanamachi, but she went by Freida. She was around forty, whose husband had passed, and left her with a small building of three floors. She was an avid reader but a terrible chess player. However, she loved the chance to play. She would cook for him two meals a day and a glass of wine when she would read to him. He loved the older ladies because they were always so thankful. And she was no exception. As she would read, he would always sit on her right. He said he could hear better through his left ear. He would sit close, and either have his hands on his lap or reach for the glass of wine, always just being close.

After a few weeks, she said, "Why don't you put your arm around me? I like the smell of your aftershave."

He let her win at chess. She had been using a lot of coal to keep their rooms warm while reading or playing chess. There was a delivery of coal, and she asked Jack to go down to the basement and

DAN BRIZZEE

open the chute and take in the coal. It was early, and he hadn't had a chance to shave, but he went to the task anyway. He was clad only in his flannel pajamas and bedroom slippers alone. When he returned to her apartment to start the furnace, he was shivering.

She saw him, wrapping her arms around him. "You're liable to catch your death. You're freezing." She rubbed her face against his beard.

She continued holding him. He pulled his head away. "I'm sorry."

She lay her head back a little. "I don't mind it. I kind of like it."

He leaned from side to side. "I guess I ought to go shave now."

She put her arms around his waist and pulled him against her. "Let it be a while. I like it."

He looked up, as though he was thinking. "How do you plan to have my beard rubbing up against your face all the time?"

She looked down, shuffling her feet. "If I say or do something inappropriately, tell me. I don't know how to act now."

He held her by her upper arms tenderly. "Would you like us to have a hug and share a kiss?"

She raised both her hands over her face, peeking through her fingers, and she began blinking and nodding because she was afraid to speak.

She wore a waist jacket, but he lifted her head by her chin. She looked up at him, and he kissed her lips, and they were into an embrace. He began kissing her face. She pulled him even closer.

He relaxed and stuck either hand with outstretched fingers into her hair. "I better get dressed. My pajamas got a little wet." He knew she wanted another kiss, but he turned and went to his room. He went and took a hot shower to warm back up and feel healthy again. By the time he went to breakfast, the apartments were nice and warm. She invited him to her kitchen for the morning meal. He sat at the kitchen table and waited. She brought the hot soup and heavy bread. She didn't sit down; instead, she rushed in with his hot coffee, setting it in front of him. She didn't sit across from him as usual. She sat very close, right next to him. He didn't react much, but she began pushing it. She began rubbing his inner thigh and was the one whom

62

began blushing. He slurped the last of his soup. Then he turned and stared at her, and she stared back, not knowing how to react. He took her face in his hands and gave her such a French kiss that she nearly passed out. He started kissing her face and neck. She put her head back and mused, as though she was having a dream. He dug his fingers into her hair, and she awoke with her eyes wide open.

He finished his coffee, pushed his chair back, and stood up. "I'm going out. I'll be back in a couple of hours."

She continued to sit at the kitchen table with her hands cradling the warm soup bowl in her hands. Her almost white blond hair was sticking up or out in every direction. She sat bleary-eyed, wondering what happened. She began to contrive scenarios, in which she could have more of that feeling of euphoria and even more and longer.

He was on his way to the telegram office. He would send a coded message to Calais. It started. The presents were wrapped with care. It was actually about David and his family, hoping to holiday in Paris. The girls were much prettier there. He asked the clerk for the form booklet, filled out the form, and showed his identification.

The clerk sent the telegram. "It may take a couple of hours."

Jack sat down on a bench. "I'll wait."

The answer came back in less than ten minutes. The clerk wrote it out and handed it to Jack. He asked for the other copy and the carbon.

The clerk seemed bemused. "I am not authorized to give those out."

"I'm waiting for my girlfriend. I'll wait in here because it is cold outside."

Two trains pulled in from different directions. The clerk grabbed two bags and ran out the door. "Don't touch anything while I'm gone."

"I won't touch anything, but Mr. Ronson might. He pulled his Ronson butane lighter from his pocket. He held it like a pistol, using the igniter like a trigger, and shot a flame, almost seven feet that caught the clerk's precious form booklet, turning it to a cinder. As he walked out onto the wooden sidewalk, he lit his copy and held it until it fell apart.

He caught a cab at the corner. "Take me around the block, a couple of times, and let me off where you picked me up." He stepped out onto the snow and walked around the corner to his apartment. He ambled up the stairs and rang the bell to her flat. The door opened, and he stood waiting. She washed and curled her hair, tight to her head.

She waved her hand low like a broom. "Come on in, doll. Did you get all your business done?"

He noticed her new hairdo, black form-fitting sequined dress, and red high heels. But he didn't mention it. "Yeah, I sent some telegrams." He ambled into the living room and sat on the couch. "What did you do while I was gone?"

She followed him into the living room and struck a pose. "What do you think?"

He looked up, nodded his approval. "Where have you been keeping that?"

She gathered the skirt of her dress, pulling it well above her knees, and sat in the chair across from him, making sure that he could see her nylons and garters. "They all came today."

He leaned forward. "Do you have an engagement?"

She looked away. "No, I just wanted you to see that I could change my appearance for you."

"Well, let me see. I believe there is an opera this weekend."

She stood and lowered the hem of her dress. "Would you take me?"

"Yes, I will take you, but you better take that dress off and hang it until next weekend."

She started for the bedroom but stopped. "Jack, will you come unzip me? I'm sure I won't be able to reach the back."

He followed her into the bedroom. He unzipped her, and the dress slid away. She put it on the hanger, pushed the straps of the slip off her shoulders, and let it fall to the floor. She picked it up and hung it in front of the dress. She hung them in the closet and stepped back before Jack, sitting and waiting.

She dropped the straps of her brassier. "I guess it is time for you to see all of me."

He stood up and walked into the kitchen. He was ambivalent. Changing his mind, he ambled into the living room and sat on the couch. She changed hurriedly into her nightgown and robe, not bothering to put on her slippers. She rushed to the kitchen. But not finding him there, she looked around franticly. She grabbed the back of a kitchen chair, using it to steady herself and stood up straight. Looking at the closed door that would open to the living room, she tried to summon her courage to barge through it—no, but to squirm or crawl through it. She accepted the latter, and pushing the door to form a crack, she peeked through, and seeing Jack sitting with his head in his hands, she continued through the door, prepared to grovel at any second. Jack sensed her presence and turned to see her almost next to him but continued mum. She dropped to her knees, placing her hands on his thigh with her head weakly bowed.

She choked and cleared her throat. "Jack, I'm sorry if I grieved you or gave you distress. I just don't know how to do it or what to do. I surely don't want to drive you away."

He thought he might stroke her hair, but she might take that poorly. He reached for her arms and pulled her up, guiding her to his lap. He kissed each of her cheeks. "I didn't want it to be like that. Just let it happen."

She pressed her face in between his neck and shoulder. "I don't know how to be voluptuous or how to entice you. I make foolish mistakes, maybe because I don't have the experience."

"Our relationship is different. You will just have to let it happen."

She looked up at him. "Will you kiss me like that again?"

She kept looking to him. He leaned to her and kissed her long and deep. It began to happen, and she reawakened her desire. But he kept the promise to himself.

She slid off his lap, sitting next to him. "What do you think of my brow?"

He was a bit stymied because he was unaware that a brow was synonymous with the protrusion of the breasts.

"I'll have to look that one up," he admitted.

"It is the sticking out of my bosoms," she spouted.

They both chuckled.

He rustled around. "I'm going to the kitchen. I'll set up the chessboard if you would care to challenge." They played on the kitchen table.

He was setting up the pieces, as she strode in. She turned, facing to his right, opened her robe, pulled the sides back, and stuck out her chest. "Which is it sticking out or slanted?"

"More than that. They are plump and perky." He scowled.

She giggled and sat down. "Accept my challenge?"

The games went into the late night.

The weekend came, and so did the opera. He remembered his promise to her. In fact, on a business trip that day, he stopped and bought her a corsage for that event.

They were finding solace and succor in each other between the operas. Freida was beginning to know how to act around him. If she desired him to do something, she would open the way for him to take what he wanted, which would turn out to be what she wanted in the beginning. It was imperative that she should never ask him about his business or where he went. As for her, the subject never came up. It happened on the evening of the final opera. Of course, he brought her a corsage, and they enjoyed the opera. It was the best. Arriving home, they walked into the living room, and as usual, Freida asked him to unzip her dress, which he did, and she went to the bedroom to change. She returned and joined Jack on the couch and had a glass of wine. They began passionate kissing and caressing. Freida's robe flared open and exposed her bare bosoms. She drew Jack's face to her breast. He looked up at her as she made gestures with her lips, all the while pressing her breast toward his lips. He finally gave in and took the nipple into his mouth and began to sup. She lay her head back and indulged in musing to dream of things never to be attained. While she was gone, he leaned back to see the nipple, around an inch and a half long and as big around as a man's thumb and whiter than her flesh. He knew that this action was a presage to fornication. He sat up and closed her robe. She looked at him and blinked several times. He kissed her as a kiss of goodbye, but she clung on to him wanting more. He knew that if he were to linger, he might break his vow. Freida was German, and he knew she would fare well.

He went to bed and was gone early the next morning. At eight five, he was on a train heading for Luxembourg with luggage ahead in Amsterdam. He bought a cup of coffee before boarding. He began to read *Odysseus* in Greek.

A big dark-haired woman sitting across from him asked. "What is it about?"

"You might say it is about his travels."

"Will you read it to us?" she asked in German.

"The German will take some time, but I can translate it faster in French."

"*Mais oui*, French."

He began reading in French. The woman leaned against the partition at the end of the seat. Soon, she fell asleep. It was like a lullaby. He was becoming drowsy himself. He slipped his book into his pouch, closed the flap, and pulled the strap tight over his shoulder. He leaned his head against the window frame and closed his eyes but not to sleep. The train stopped, and the big woman got off. They passed into Belgium. They would pause for around ten minutes to take on water and passengers; the conductor announced. Jack stood up before his seat to stretch his legs. He lifted the flap on his pouch and pulled out another book. He glanced at the title and sat back down. The title was *I Claudius*. A young woman passed and took a seat at the back end of the car. Another woman passed and went to the same end of the car, stopped, and looked around but found no accommodation. She huffed and walked to the opposite end of the car, passing Jack again.

He looked at his book and began thumbing through it. Finding nothing at the other end, she returned and stood in front of Jack. "Is that seat next to you taken, or are you saving it for someone?"

He picked up his valise and stowed it under his chair. "I am terribly sorry. I guess I wasn't paying attention."

She sat with her handbag on her lap. "I suppose not. Wasn't that rude?"

He continued searching the pages of his book. "I supposed so." He didn't look up.

"What is it you're fiddling with anyway?"

Then he looked up. "It's a Roman story." He noticed her handsome face, and she wore a hat with plumes, not overdone.

"I'm sorry I was so trite. I was getting frustrated." She leaned over toward him to see the open page. "What sort of language is that?"

He lay the pages open. "This is Latin."

"Can you read it for me?"

"*A coup sur, a gauche.*"

"Are you tricking me? Is it the joke?"

He looked hard at the book. "It's about a king who forces his wife to give up her baby because she is not a son for the king. She tells him that the child is at the bottom of the river, but she left the child on the stoop in a basket in the early morning."

"What a morbid tale!"

"Yes, but that is not the worst of it. The child was left on the stoop, in the basket, at early morn. So the whoremonger would take her and raise her to be a bawd. At least, she would be alive, proving that no one has a choice in life."

"That is depressing but most likely true."

He closed the book and put it back in his pouch. "It's probably true and definitely depressing."

She slid a little closer and leaned in on him. "I need some succor after that."

He put his arm around her, and she snuggled into him. Her plume wafted before his face. "Shouldn't we introduce ourselves?"

"Okay." She leaned away just a little. "My name is Erma."

"I'm Jack. What shall we talk about now?"

She sat up straight. "Where are you going in Brussels?"

"I'm supposed to meet some people at the central train station, but I'm not sure they will be there to meet me."

"What will you do there, or will you go on to Amsterdam?"

"I'll look for something in Brussels. If I were to go on to Amsterdam, I might get into trouble. I'll lay that I can work in a hotel. There is always extra money to be made if it is swank." He didn't ask about it.

"I'm going to spend some time in Brussels, then on to the Hague, or Amsterdam. Might you advise me on a hotel? It sounds like you have been here before."

She began to perceive him as trustworthy.

"I was born and grew up in Brussels. I can show you around. Wouldn't that be swell?"

"I will want to ask you some questions, would you mind?"

"*No,* I wouldn't mind. I can leave anytime I wish."

"May I ask you a question now?"

"Okay, go ahead."

With that, she acted with boldness to measure his trustfulness.

"May I use you for a pillow? I would like a nap on the way."

"À bras ouverts." (With open arms.) He raised his arm to the back of the seat.

At that point, he determined to give her solace and succor.

She laid up against his side and rested her head on his shoulder and went off to dreamworld. And she went so quickly he was amazed. He laid his head against the window and began to muse. He roused himself, and Erma grabbed for her hat, but Jack removed it because the feather was tickling his nose. As she sat up, she saw that he had it on his lap. She looked at him. He twitched his nose. She understood. They gathered their things and left the car. On the platform, they found their baggage and ambled to the main door, followed by two attendants.

Jack looked up and down the street. "Erma, can you whistle?"

She looked him up and down. "What on earth for?"

"I've seen it done to call a cab." One of the attendants whistled, and a cab appeared. They loaded the luggage into the cab.

Jack opened the cab's door.

"Are you going with me?" Erma crawled in.

"I guess I am. I'll lay. You have me set." Jack hopped in, and they were off. "You are the navigator," Jack quipped.

She turned to Jack. "What is our budget?"

"We will need two bedrooms and two baths."

She leaned forward to the cabbie and said, "La Miracle Wonder."

The cabbie nodded.

She sat back squaring her shoulders. "May I take it that you are a wealthy man?"

"I would prefer to ask questions and answer once we are settled in a hotel."

They arrived at the front of their hotel. Jack opened the door and stepped out. He held the door for Erma and extended a hand to her, helping her out to stand, holding her out of the swing of the door as he closed it. The cabbie unloaded the cab and stood waiting by the luggage.

Jack held up a five-franc note. "Please bring them into the lobby."

The cabbie grabbed the note and hustled the baggage into the lobby. As soon as Jack signed in using his full name, they were treated like royalty with a four-room suite and a large sunroom. The bellhops were summoned, and they were shown to their suite.

As they stepped into the foyer, she removed her hat and placed it on a small table, close to the door. They went into a sitting room. He pulled off his jacket and lay it over the back of the couch.

He stood before two chairs that faced each other. "Let's sit here." He sat on the one to his right.

Erma was standing behind the other chair with her hand clasped over the top of the back of it. She stepped around to the front of it and sat down. She sat with a quizzical look on her face.

Jack thought, *I need to get a look at the whole of her.*

He looked to the foyer. "Will you go get your hat, please?"

She smiled, spun out of her chair, and marched to the foyer, gingerly picked up her hat, and returned to her chair, placing her hat on her lap, and smiled a big toothy smile. He applauded and smiled back.

He had taken her measure from her heavy auburn hair, cut short at the shoulder, with a curl on the end to her dark-brown dress, with pleated shirt and buttoned top and shiny brown slip-on shoes. She had a nice little swing in her gait.

He shuffled in his chair and settled back. "Your turn."

She cleared her throat and swallowed. "Are you wealthy? And how wealthy? How educated?" She sat back and waited.

"I was given a thirty-six-month tour of Europe paid for by my mother that includes a stipend. I'm not sure how much that is. I simply ask, and it comes. I earned a PhD at UCLA in California."

He hunched forward on his chair. "What is your education? What sort of work have you done? What is your age?"

She lowered her head and wagged it back and forth slightly. "I did not get to go to school because, we had to pay to go to school, and my papa was a gambler, so we moved around all the time. Mama died when she gave birth to my youngest sister. There were four of us girls. I was just thirteen when Papa sold me to get a big stake for a game in Paris. He said he would come and buy me back when he wins a big pot, but I never saw him again. That is where I learned to count money. I think I'll be thirty-seven next September." She kept hanging her head. She sniffed, straightened up, and sat back. "Why are you here in Europe? You seem to be after something. Why did you pick me up or befriend me? What do you expect from me?"

"As I said before, my mother sent me to Europe to find a nice Jewish wife. But I am not ready to marry yet, and I cannot ask a woman to wait until I am ready. I will just smell the roses as long as I am in the garden. Your second and third questions may be a little combined. It seems that we chose each other, but for my part, I wanted someone to travel with. And second, I felt empathy for you and chose to give you solace and succor. Finally, I want you to be my pert, not an empty hole."

"You seem fairly educated. How did that come about? Have you had children? Would you mind traveling?"

"I am afraid I don't know the meanings of those two words—*solace* and *succor*."

"They mean that I am going to console you and help, aid, and relieve you."

"Do you mean that you planned this?"

"Sort of."

"Will you please answer my questions?"

"I think it may be a long story. Are you sure you want to hear it?"

"Yes, time is of no consequence."

She clamped her lips together and looked to the side. "It is hard for me to recall, but I will try to stay composed. It was 1914 when Papa took me to the brothel. I was not aware of why I was there. We stood around outside for some time. I was wearing a simple little dress. A big man came out and showed us inside. It was very strange inside. We were ushered upstairs and into a large room with many windows. There were several overstuffed chairs and an enormous desk. A big woman sat at the desk. We stood waiting. The woman stood up, 'What do you have to sell?'

"Papa said, 'This one here. She is easily coursed and of age, fourteen years. I am asking fifteen hundred francs.'

"The woman stepped around to the front of the desk. 'Take off that filthy dress. I will see what I am buying.'

"Papa pulled my dress over my head. It was then that I knew what she was buying.

"She moved forward, pushing my head back. 'Open your mouth. Let me see your teeth.' She turned to Papa. 'Twelve hundred, no more. See the clerk at the front door.'

"Papa stuffed my dress, wadded up under his arm. 'I will come back for you as soon as I win a big pot.' I never saw him again though.

"I was taken to a room, which turned out to be the attic. It was very cold at night. Some of the bawds came to console me but mostly to convince me that they would work me into it, saying that they would ease me into it. I finally conceded after a few weeks and started with ten lays a day and night. Eventually, I realized that the more lays I would allow, the more money, so I was doing twenty a day. Some times more. But after some time passed, I began doing extra for my favorites. Then one evening, a special one presented me with a large bouquet. I took the bouquet and dumped it in the wastebasket.

"Crossing my legs, I said, 'I will do you extra special if you bring me a big bouquet of folding cash.'

"He must have spread the word because the cash came rolling in. There was so much that I had to find a place to hide it because if there was a raid, the cops would confiscate any money they found on you. I found a loose floorboard under a foot on my bed. So I moved the foot a little, and the board popped up, but I had to pull it up a little more and slip the money in out of sight. Pushing the board down and sliding the foot over that board, I concealed my stash. I was almost twenty when the Great War came, and most of my specials went off to fight. Business became slow, and no fun at all. Then the armistice was signed, and the party began again. A few of my specials returned, but it was not the same. They would rather spend time with their grandchildren than with the bawds. I was in my early twenties, and I got tired of weekly alum douches and rough-and-tumble men. So I wanted a change, and I snuck out with a suitcase full of money and caught a train to Munich. I made some deposits and decided to get educated. I found a Catholic school run by an order of nuns. I attended eight one-hour classes daily, except Sunday, for six years. I am fluent, read, and compose in English, French, German, Latin, and Greek. They did not offer calculus, but I know trigonometry. I also took five science classes. I will be your courtesan or pert, inside and outside, day or night. I will be a mother."

Jack squirmed to get comfortable in his chair. "I will not take you as a courtesan because I have taken a vow, but a pert inside will be fine. A mother will fit well into my plans."

She popped her lips. "What is your vow about?"

He bit his lip. "I will not commit fornication or its precursor."

"So no lovemaking?"

"Anything, except sexual intercourse, is permissible."

"Can we kiss and hug, or will you press my breast?"

"All totally permissible. Say, do you have an outfit that is more demure?"

"Yes, why?"

"I am getting hungry. Shouldn't we go to dinner?"

"Yes, and I know the perfect place."

The diner was packed, so they took a table out front. A waiter came by.

"Two Pernods," Jack quipped.

She slid her chair closer to Jack, leaning to him. "Can I have a sonly kiss?"

He chortled. "Don't be trite."

"Give it to Mama." He kissed her cheek.

"You are going to get a spanking when we get home."

Under his breath, he uttered, "Erma."

"When we get home, I'll pull your pants down and spank you good."

He laid his head on the table and snickered weakly, then sat up erect, and glared at her.

She laughed out loud. "Aren't we having a fine time?"

The waiter came with their drinks.

He smirked, "You know, little girls shouldn't drink this."

She drew a long sip, placed the glass on the table. "What would you know of little girls?"

He took a drink and looked over the rim of the glass. "So you want to spar, is it?"

"Not really. I was just having a joke." She chortled.

The waiter came out.

"What is yours?" asked Jack.

"The rack of lamb sounds good. Can we split it?"

"That will be fine," quipped Jack.

She drew a mouthful and swallowed. "I am having many great ideas today, aren't I?"

Five courses appeared with two bottles of wine, white and red. They drank the wine Roman but scavenged the flesh from the bone as though a barbarian. Their table cleared; they settled with finishing the red.

He guzzled the last of his wine, nearly choking. "A horse cab," he blurted.

Looking away to the carriage on the street, Erma quipped, "Yes, it is a horse-drawn carriage."

They got to their feet. Jack dropped some folding money on the table; they raced to the cab. As she climbed in, he lifted her by the elbow. Once she was settled, he slipped off his coat and tossed it up to her. She took it and lay it across her lap. He climbed up and settled in next to her. She leaned forward, allowing him to slip his arm around her shoulder. He pulled her to himself, clamping her in, under his wing, as it were.

He leaned forward slightly. "Around the park until—"

The driver answered, "At your will, sir."

They passed some shops that were just now closing into a grove of trees, then under a bridge. The passage was long, and the horse slowed his gait.

He put his fingers under her chin, to have her looking up. "It is a little dark. May I kiss you?"

"Remember, I was a French bawd. Fellatio was a frequently used tool. I wash and rinse my mouth day and night, forever, but I can't clean it from my mind." She hung her head.

He touched under her chin. She laid her head back as if it were a command. He pulled her to him and kissed her. His tongue touched her lips, and they magically opened. He dove in as far as possible and held, feeling her hot breath on his face. Letting her free, he kissed her cheeks several times.

He sat back, looking at her. "Now that is what I think of that. Yesterday is yesterday, and never again."

She laid her head against this chest. They rolled along at a smooth and rolling gate. Dusk was coming on, and a light mist was in the air. She handed him his coat thinking that he would put it on. But he had her lean forward and put it over her shoulders. The horse came to a stop and shuddered. Jack climbed down to the street and lifted his hand to Erma to draw her down from the carriage. There was a nicely lit café just up the street from their hotel. They went in to have a nightcap. There were two waiters—one behind the bar and the other serving. They sat at a table away from the window. Erma took off her hat and placed it on the table.

The serving waiter came over and asked, "What's yours?"

Jack looked at Erma. "Will you have cognac?"

She gazed at the couple sitting before the window. "Of course, darling. Say, notice that girl's skirt? It's slit up so it shows her underpants."

"When did you become such a prude?"

"I swear, you need a spanking."

"Are you saying I am a bad boy?"

"Well, you can be at home."

The cognac was served. There were two cookies on either saucer and a small pitcher of Selzer.

"I think we will take you shopping tomorrow."

"I think that will be splendid. My outfits are not very conservative or demure enough."

"You must select a new hat, as well—maybe two or three."

"I like the way you think." She snapped a cookie and poured a little Selzer on her cognac.

She finished the Selzer on his cognac.

He stirred with a swizzle and took a drink. "It is well past dark. Perhaps we should stroll toward our hotel?"

"I was hoping you would take a little more time laying out your plans for me."

"Okay, notwithstanding your shopping trip, you should move any funds you hold in Germany to Switzerland because any funds in Germany will be stolen. We will go to Austria, then to Greece, and finally home to the USA."

"Are you going to take me home with you? How?"

"Don't worry about how. I will see to that. I don't want you to stay in New York. I'll get you settled in California." She wanted to hug and kiss him, but she was still mother.

He stood, giving her his hand, to rise. She snatched her hat, placing it on after stepping out the door. They ambled toward the hotel. As they walked along, they noticed a chill in the air. But when they stepped into the lobby of their hotel, they noticed how warm and cozy it was. They made a quick trip, up the stairs, and into their flat, but that put a chill into them because apparently the heater had not been turned on.

He grabbed her and began rubbing her back. "I'll have a load of coal delivered tomorrow. I believe that will remedy the situation. However, tonight, we have an immediate problem."

From his trunk, he produced an enormous comforter, which he spread out on his bed. He began undressing. "Darling, get undressed and jump in under the comforter. We can use body heat to keep each other warm." He slid under, and they snuggled up together. They both lay on their left side.

She pushed her rump into his lower abdomen, searched for his right hand, pulling it over her under arm. She led it to her breast, and he clutched it tenderly. She breathed a sigh of relief, and they took to sleep.

He woke to Erma kissing his face and neck. "Are you awake yet?"

He leaned up. "I think so."

She pushed him back down. "I want to give you something back." She lifted him to her kiss, but his lips were puckered closed. She raised back a little. "Darling, you have to let me in."

He blinked twice. "What?"

Before he finished the word, she dove in. It was absolute delight, but when she began to hum in a low hum, it was more than he could take. It gave him an erogenous tic feeling, but he held his forbearance. She began kissing his face again. He pulled her close to him and embraced her tight.

He kissed her back. "I think we better get dressed."

She rolled over onto him. "Let me feel you just a while longer."

He rubbed her back for a little while. "Enough, I'm getting hungry."

She kissed him and rolled off and trotted to the bath. He determined he would be the first to wake from then on. They took care of the morning necessities, dressed, and took the lift to the lobby. They ambled out into the cool morning air. Standing on the sidewalk, Jack hailed a cab, and they were off for a morning of shopping. Returning at 3:00 PM, they would postpone the trip to Germany until the next week. However, they did gather four garment bags, three new pieces of luggage containing four pairs of shoes, including nylon, and garter belts. *Oh,* and three new flamboyant hats.

The funds did get transferred to Switzerland and converted to Swiss francs. They made their trip to Austria and arranged a small flat for either of them. Erma busied herself scrounging the cities, for eligible young Jewish girls for liaisons with Jack, but the families usually sent their oldest daughter, which meant that they would be past their prime by the time that Jack would get around to them. There were a couple—ages eleven or twelve—but the parents would not get out of harm's way. Erma and Jack left Austria for Greece in spring 1938. They sailed from Croatia on the Adriatic Sea to the port at Athens. There were few Jewish families to be found. Another problem was that Greek woman were not as big as he had envisioned. Quite the contrary, they seemed small of frame and timid in actions. The young women would strike up a conversation with Mother but seemed to be afraid of Jack. The two of them sat at the cafes and went to the beach at midday. On a particular August afternoon, they lay on the patio, sunbathing and drinking gin and tonic.

Jack sat up. "Erma?"

She leaned up on her right elbow. "What is it, Jack?"

He pulled his knees up and wrapped his forearms around them. "Say, if you pull that knot out of your hair, how far down your back will the curls fall?"

She shuffled and leaned back on her forearm. "I'd have to sit on my rump, like you are, to do that."

"Well, then what do you say?"

"Okay." She sat up and pulled the knot out, and the curls fell past her shoulder blades. She had a quizzical look on her face. "Please, darling, will you rub me down? I am sweating, so it feels somewhat sticky."

"Of course, sweetheart. Lie back down and pull your hair up."

He rubbed her back, then toweled her off with a damp, cool towel.

She rolled over. "Now my front. Try not to get us aroused."

He rubbed very delicately in sensitive areas. "My libido has been stuck in neutral for years. But the smell of your sweat is like an aphrodisiac to me."

He wrung the ice water out of the towel and proceeded to spread it over her breasts and abdomen. He laid it on slowly; she shivered but rose, bracing herself on her elbows. "There are a couple of towns that we haven't tried yet."

"How far apart must they be then?"

She sat up. "Remember, Greece is about the size of New York State."

"Do you have some names?"

"I don't think I can do it all from memory, but I will put a list together this afternoon."

They went to their favorite little café for a fish lunch. Mother complained all the way to and back, "Why do I have to wear this halter top? I see plenty of women around here going topless."

"Those women are not eating at the restaurant."

"This fabric scratches my nipples."

"Just leave it on until we get to our place."

As soon as they walked in through the door, she zipped it off. "Look, I'm leaving my shorts on." She went to the desk and jotted down some names of towns. She began with Edessa, north maybe by train; Komotini, also maybe by a train access; Larisa, in the middle of nowhere; Corfu, isolated on an island.

"We will need to spend at least a week in each town. I'll lay it that each one will have a festival."

Edessa was on the rail, and there were three dances and lambs on a spit. He was visited by seven girls the first week. Four were brought by their mothers. The others were exhibited by their sisters. The sisters were most kind, while the mothers were selling a side of beef. The girls would show any part asked by Jack or the attendants. Most of the girls were heavy, with sturdy bodies, and free of moles or acne. The others were trim and seemed of a good demeanor, with a submissive nature. They all had either dark-brown or auburn wavy hair, reaching to their waist. Most were planning on eight to ten children, as soon as possible, and a larger number of male infants.

Jack found that the morals in the north were somewhat different compared to how it appeared in the more affluent areas like Athens. The girls were perfectly willing to share a husband. If there was a family involved and that subject came up, there was a lot of giggling, but they didn't seem to mind. He was told by a mother in Komotini that it was expected that a husband should keep however many wives he had in line, who are submissive, with corporal punishment used if need be. However, he noticed the appearance of the mothers and grandmothers was the result of deleterious treatment by their spouses. But the girls were in fine shape.

It was almost a month and a half before they arrived in Corfu. The women were fair and little taller and amenable to their presentation. He was stymied because of their beauty and graciousness. He wanted to take them all but could not take any. He simply could not decide. He took a few names and locations, thinking that he might return. He was thinking of how difficult it might be to select the proper wife in the USA. And these girls had been trained all their lives just for that purpose. He would try to return. He determined that these girls were built for having babies and predisposed to nurturing them. Plus, they would be enamored for their husband.

Erma and Jack sailed from Moraitika to Plataria, then a rickety bus into Athens. They were stuck in Athens, four days, waiting for a steamer that would take them to Gibraltar. They took their time with fresh fish, lamb, and ouzo, with fiesta into the night. They were coming upon the end side of thirty-eight. The weather was changing, so they were anxious to make a run for the open sea. Once north of Portugal, heading for the Isle of Man, then cutting east to Liverpool. Taking the train from Liverpool to London, they had a wonderful time sharing a spacious compartment. Arriving in London on January 12, Jack rushed to the ticket office. He chartered the next available seats on the Boeing 307 Stratoliner, not yet available in the USA, but scheduled to land in New York on January 31, 1939. That would mean that there would be plenty of time for preparation and sightseeing. It would also afford an opportunity for frivolity. This would be their last dance.

Jack showed her the tickets. "You aren't afraid to fly, are you?"

"I don't know. I have never flown before."

"I haven't either. I suppose it will be a new experience for both of us."

The 307 boasted a pressurized cabin, allowing it to cruise along above ten thousand feet, above weather troubles, hence the name, Stratoliner, indicating into the stratosphere and also hinting at the mighty Jetstream or a great tailwind. He was afraid that Mother would try to cause a great conflagration, so when they arrived over an hour ahead of time, they caught a DC-3 up to Chicago and on to San Francisco. They hosteled it at Sausalito. They had been racing the sun, so it was late morning when they drove into Santa Rosa. They met with a realtor who showed them several pieces but finally came to a parcel of six hundred acres with limestone outcroppings. A deal was struck, and they returned to Sausalito.

Jack laid out his plan to Erma. That afternoon, they met Nick at the Transamerica Building. He brought a well-known vintner from the area to help her get started in the wine-making business. Nick agreed to handle the financial end. Jack kissed Erma on her forehead.

"You are a lovely lady, and you are free to run now." He walked out and couldn't look back. He got in the back seat of a waiting car. It went up the street. The car turned onto Lincoln and started down. He was sure he lost something.

Traveling south on a partially completed highway, they crossed into Santa Clara and into the university. Rushing to his office, he called for a typist. He began putting his report together in his head.

A couple of minutes later, the typist walked through the open door of his office. "It smells and feels somewhat stuffy in here." He pushed a window up as far as it would go.

"It smells like it does because it has been closed up for three years." The typist chortled. He rolled in a piece of typing paper.

Jack began dictating. "We'll need twelve copies of this."

Jack was carrying out more than a search for a future wife. It seemed like a perfectly plausible cover. While in France, he found that the French upper military leaders had been mostly disbanded, and the army was a mere shadow of its former self. The Germans had embedded officials, supporters of the socialist agenda, on the side of the Germans. France would be absolutely defenseless. In Berlin, the propaganda was subliminally advocating a reemergence of the Fatherland, taking back all the areas lost through World War I and the Treaty of Versailles. Luxemburg, Amsterdam, Poland, and Greece were in a threatened position. There were German officers and squads in all those areas. It was meant to appear that the officers were on holiday, but what was the explanation for the squads? It seemed that the Germans had their eyes on the Mediterranean and Africa. In Berlin, there were whispers of South America.

The presentation ended. "It sounds like war, but Congress will not act," quipped Warmerdam, a congressman.

"They are going to let Berlin get everything in their back pocket. They are building factories left and right, and they aren't making dollies." Jack chortled.

Barns asked, "What about Japan? But I've heard that the negotiations are stalling all the time. What about the Japs in the Pacific? They are everywhere."

Jack ambled to the door. "We will just have to wait on Congress unless something big happens. I'll see you guys soon. Got to go. Bye."

He had the driver let him off in front of a used-car lot in San Jose, California. He picked up a 1935 Ford. He chose that make and model because he didn't want to appear rich or too well-off. Next, he bought a pair of chords and a plaid short-sleeved shirt. Feeling dressed down, he went to a high school hangout, the Puma's den. That just didn't seem to work out too well. Feeling a little letdown, he walked around the small town, and soon, he was feeling hungry, so he stopped at a burger place, ordering a footlong hot dog, fries, and a soda. The waitress who brought his food didn't have any more customers.

So she asked, "Are you new around here?"

"Actually, I just came down from San Jose. Name's Jack."

"I'm Peggy. Whatcha doing in Cowtown?"

"Well, I'm kind of looking for a girl."

"Well, I'm a girl."

"Yeah, but you're working."

"Well, there's going to be about twenty girls showing up here before you can finish your lunch. Maybe you will find that girl in them. If not, I'll be available after two."

"I'll keep you in mind. How old are you anyway?"

"Don't you know you ain't supposed to ask a girl her age? I just turned sixteen."

"You are so young. Why aren't you in school?"

"My daddy died when I was a junior, so I fell behind, and I quit. I need to help my mama with money also."

"You say you're off at two, huh?"

"Yeah, but here come the students. They get lunch at twelve or one. They have to be back in class by one or two. Hey, guys, this is Jack. He's from San Jose."

Jack finished his lunch, while the students made their orders. Someone put a nickel in the jukebox, and Jack was dancing with three girls at the same time. A couple of the guys jumped in, but the time went so fast that Jack didn't get a chance to chat with any of the girls. It was almost two thirty by the time Peggy came around from the back of the hamburger stand. She was carrying a half-eaten hot dog.

Jack rolled down his window. "Is that one of the benefits of working here?"

Peggy was chewing as she swaggered toward him, sitting in the driver's seat of the Ford. She swallowed hard and leaned against the front fender. "I took it out after Mell left. He locks up the soda pop before he leaves, so I couldn't get one, without paying for it." She put her left foot on the running board.

"Why don't we run over to the drugstore, and I get you a cherry Coke?"

"We only met just before lunch. I don't know if I can trust you. I can't take rides from strangers."

"Your name is Peggy, and I am Jack. See, we aren't strangers anymore."

She pointed the half-eaten hot dog at him. "If you try something funny, I'll kick you where it hurts." She wrapped up the hot dog and climbed in on the passenger's side.

He had to go out on the front street and go around the block to be going in the right direction to be able to vertical park in front of Grave's Drugs.

He knew it was coming. By the second right-hand turn, she began shouting questions. "Where are we going?"

He drove up in front of Grave's Drugs.

She looked over the dashboard and out the windshield. "You weren't lying."

Virtue being the better part of valor, he kept his mouth shut.

"Let's get your cherry Coke." He closed the door and stepped up on the sidewalk.

Peggy slammed her door. "I'd like a cup."

When they came out to the car, she had a cup with a straw. Once in the car, she unwrapped her hot dog that she now had to unwind because she was squeezing it so hard while going around the block.

"Can I finish my hot dog before we start?" she asked.

He leaned back, raising his right arm to the top of the seat back. "Do you want me to take you home when you're finished?"

She slurped her Coke. "I do like the taste of this cherry."

He pushed the key in and hit the ignition. "I better move. I don't want to get a ticket." He backed out and pulled onto the avenue. "I better get you home."

She leaned forward. "Go left at the light. I live down that street."

He went over the railroad tracks, passed a couple large buildings, the gymnasium, and the swimming pool, all on the left side going east. Ahead on the right, he saw a large vacant lot.

She pointed at that lot. "Stop at that lot. I can walk from there."

He looked around, out the front window. "Where's your house?"

"It's across that ditch. You can't get to my house from here. Thanks for the cherry Coke."

He watched as she did a balancing act on a board used to cross the ditch. He looked past the ditch, but all he saw were three ramshackle broken-down shacks. He kept watching her until she climbed up the steps of the second house. He made a U-turn at the corner and headed back downtown.

The next morning, just past nine, he entered the secretaries' office to ask the particulars concerning Peggy's predicament. They said that all they could say was that Sergeant Dobbs was killed in a training exercise while in the Navy. Jack wrote a letter to the comandante at San Diego. The upshot, all death benefits, back pay, and retirement pay was forthcoming.

He stopped in for lunch at the Burger Shack. Peggy slid his burger in front of him. "What have you been up to?"

He reached for a napkin. "Do you know how many students are in this class, right now? Can I get a Pepsi?"

She set the Pepsi on the table and popped the cap with a church key. "That'll be ten cents."

He sipped the Pepsi. "They're a nickel, across the street in the machine."

She pointed the church key at him. "I already opened it, and you already sipped it, so pay up. Mell's gotta make a profit."

He took a bite of the burger, holding it in his cheek. "Why're you being so cruel to me?"

She stands with her fists on her hips. "You better finish your burger. Your prey will be coming soon."

He wiped his mouth took a sip. "Why did you have to say it like that?"

She stepped back to the counter. She went in the side door and stood behind the counter, waiting for the students coming down the sidewalk. She purposefully wouldn't look in Jack's direction. Finishing his Pepsi, he put a nickel in the jukebox, and while dancing with a couple of the girls, he mentioned that he would be over at Grave's Drugstore, a little after three, and he might furnish cherry Cokes, for anyone who would care to engage in friendly conversation. At three fifteen, two girls came through the door and spied Jack, sitting in a booth, enjoying an ice-cream cone.

The two girls approached him. "Can we sit together on the other side?"

Jack, trying to keep up with the melting ice cream, replied, "However you wish."

Janice, a blond, asked, "Can I have an ice-cream cone instead?"

The other, with dark short hair, said, "I would love a cherry Coke." She went by Judy.

Jack turned toward the counter. "Bring a cherry Coke and a double scoop of vanilla ice cream on a cone. Put the cone on the hanger.

"That'll be two bits," called the soda jerk.

"Bring it. Your tip is waiting," quipped Jack.

Jack had a quarter, topped with a dime, and the attendant smiled. "Thank you, sir."

The girls took their Cokes and cone.

Jack pulled a napkin from the holder and handed it to Janice. "Janice, what is your major?"

"I'm in business."

"What do you plan to do with it?"

"I guess I can be a secretary."

"What is your grade average?"

"I'm not sure. Does that matter?"

"You do want to graduate, don't you?"

"Of course, I want to be able to get a job."

"What kind of job?"

"In an office, maybe."

"Have you ever thought about getting married?"

"No, I think that will just happen."

"What sort of man will you marry?"

"I don't know. Ask Judy something."

"I am sorry if I caused you anxiety."

"You just asked me a lot of questions that I should know the answers to, but I just don't know the answers to any for sure."

"How old are you?"

"I'll be sixteen in June."

"How's that Coke, Judy?"

"Swell."

"And what is your major?"

"Home economics."

"How are your grades?"

"I think I have B+ because my math is holding me back."

"Can you make gravy without lumps?"

"Yes, but my biscuits are light and flaky."

"Would you ever get married?"

"I would if I could find a good man who is trustworthy."

"I am afraid you're saying a lot or more than can be delivered."

"Do you play an instrument?"

"Clarinet, but my old one is broken, and a new one is very expensive, and there are no extras for the band."

"We better start for home. It'll be after five before we get there."

"I can give you a ride home if you want."

"No, thanks. My mom would bust a gasket if I showed up in some strange man's car."

"I guess you're right. Is there anything I can do for you girls, to show my appreciation?"

"Could we share a cherry Coke on our way home?"

He stepped up to the counter. "Give me two cherry Cokes in cups with plastic lids and two straws."

The soda jerk made the cherry Cokes and set them on the counter. Jack flipped him a quarter. "Keep the change."

He swung around with a Coke in each hand. "Here you go. Compliments of Jack."

"*Wow!* Isn't this swell? Thanks, Jack." They rushed out the door.

He thought about a haircut, but it was too late. He walked past the corner market, turned around, stepped in through the open doors, and bought a cold soda from the machine inside. He went outside and stood, leaning against the outside wall of the market. He heard his name called.

"Jack! Hey, Jack! It's Peggy. I've got to wait on this traffic."

"You wait for the light to change," he ordered.

She stepped back behind the curb. The light changed, and she bolted across the street, almost getting hit by a right turner. She ran up and stood right in front of him.

She looked at his Pepsi. "You want some?" he quipped.

"I don't know where your mouth has been, maybe kissing one of those girls at the drugstore. They were running awful fast when they came out."

"You're just being silly now."

She gave a shallow curtsy. "I was just checking to see what you've been up to."

"*Oh!* You were spying on me, were you?"

"Not really, but when I saw those girls come flying out of Grave's Drugs, it piqued my interest."

"I notice that you aren't wearing your uniform. What is that you have on there?"

"It's my dress, just in case you might take me dancing."

"I've been checking out the dance halls around here, and they are all bars. If I were to take you in there, I'd wind up in jail. We don't want that. But right over on the next block is a Chinese restaurant, and I will buy you a plate of chow mein."

He lifted up his elbow, and she took it, and they walked arm in arm, across the street, and into the Golden Dragon.

As they ambled through the doors, there was a counter to the right with perhaps ten or twelve swivel stools before it. On the left were nine booths. A Chinese woman used her open hand to usher them to the middle booth. As they sat down, she offered them a menu.

Jack glanced at it. "We'll both have the chow mein."

Peggy handed her menu to Jack. The woman came with a pot and two cups. She sat them on the table and took the menus from Jack.

"I don't think you ordered that."

"It's green tea. It comes with the meal."

She sat back and looked at him.

He poured the two cups full. "Better let it cool a little. It's really hot."

She looked up toward the ceiling. "How long do we wait?"

"Give it a minute or two, and then try it."

"Ow! It's still hot."

Their entrées arrived, with three fried shrimps on top, with a small plate of hot mustard on the side.

"Are we supposed to eat those things?"

"Just try one. You will like it."

She nibbled on one. "It's still pretty hot."

"Try your chow mein while you let it cool a little. Your tea might be cool by now."

She sipped her tea. "That's not bad. I like this. Can I have some more?"

"The tea in the pot will be hot for a while, so let it cool as well," he warned.

"You were right about the shrimp. I really do like it."

They ate for a while.

"I'm getting really full. I don't think I want any more."

"We can talk for a while. You'll be hungry again in half an hour."

"Tell me what you know about your father's death."

She raised her hands. "Just what my mom told me. She said that he was killed by friendly fire while on maneuvers."

"And you didn't get anything from the Navy?"

"They were at the funeral, gave my mom a flag, and there was gunfire, but that was it."

"And the family wasn't offered subsistence?"

"No, that's why I had to get that crummy job. I buy eggs from a chicken farm behind our house. I have an egg in the morning and for dinner and lunch, whatever I can scam off Mell. Sometimes, it gets really hard."

He poured more tea, took a sip, and looked at her, holding the cup before his mouth, thinking of another sip, or was it about her?

"You were right. I'm a little hungry again. I'm going to eat some more. It sure feels good to be full. What are you looking at? You looked like you were in a daze."

"I was just wondering what we should do next. Aren't you finished eating?"

She guzzled the last pouring of tea. "Have you come up with an idea yet?"

"We'll get some groceries and take them to your place."

She grasped the edge of the table with both hands, leaning forward. "If you pull that trick, my mother will throw a fit."

He laid some coins on the table, next to a plate. "She'll get over it. Don't worry about it. I'll handle it."

He noticed the color of her hair, a dishwater blond. Probably the reason she cut it close to her head. She had a handsome face, not glitzy at all but appealing. She was thin, not skinny, at all. She was a helper and resourceful. She wasn't for him, but because of the way she was, he wanted to help her.

She patted his hand. "Are you dreaming again?"

He shook his head. "Let's go find a meat market."

She stood with hands on her waists, wiggling her hips. "You really know how to get to a girl's heart, doncha?"

"Let's go." And they were out the door.

At the meat market, Jack said, "I'll take that rump roast, a dozen pork chops, and that slab of bacon."

Butcher said, "I've got some nice fresh chicken."

"No, thanks. An ice box is not going to keep chicken fresh."

At the clerk, he said, "That will be two dollars and twenty-nine cents."

Peggy carried a bag, and Jack caught the other. Then they went on to a produce stand and finally the corner market. Six dollars and five cents later, with a trunk full of groceries, and on the way home stopping at the chicken farm, for two flats of eggs, that fit nicely on the back seat. Jack had taken the highway, past the canal, and into the chicken farm, then up to the house, fronted by a dirt road.

Jack popped the trunk. "Peggy, can you carry two bags?"

Peggy, grabbing two bags, replied, "You bet. I've got them."

Mama came down the steps. "What on earth?"

Jack, coming down the steps, with Peggy ahead, said, "Peg, will you close the trunk?"

"I got it."

Jack turned and stepped back into the living room. "Mom, we should have a talk right away, like now."

There were three other children in the house, hungry but in good health. Everybody was putting groceries away as Jack explained what was about to happen.

Jack pulled a kitchen chair back and asked Mama to sit. "By the end of this week, you will receive an allotment from the Navy, sufficient to buy a larger home in town that will accommodate you and your children and your first month's subsistence."

Mama began to cry.

Peggy grabbed him, hugging him. "You have made us all so happy." Even the smallest child was trying to join in on a group hug.

He grasped the back of a kitchen chair. "All these children should be in school, especially Peggy." He stepped out onto the front porch, looked at his Ford, walked to it, and drove away.

*****

He continued interviewing young women of the town, for a few weeks, but most of them had a different mindset compared to what he was looking for. Summer 1940 came, and Peggy invited him to tour their new home. After going through it, she led him to the dining room, where she invited him to sit and chat.

"I have everything made up at school, and I am going to try to graduate next June. That will be 1941. I wonder if you will come and see me graduate."

"I'm not sure what the future holds. What will you do after you graduate?"

"I don't think I'm smart enough to go to college."

"That is only a state of mind."

"If you were to stay around, I would think about being a wife."

"There are a lot of people in this world, and I'll bet there is a good and true husband out there, somewhere."

"I've never been asked to a school dance or asked to a formal. I wouldn't be able to go anyway. Those dresses are so expensive."

He stuck around, and early December, he took her to the big city and had her fitted for a couple formal dresses, and he took her to the Christmas formal. The other girls were jealous because most of the young men were asking her to dance. When the dance was over, they got in the Ford and on the way home.

She scooted closer and closer, "Jack, can we park?"

He drove to that vacant lot on the way to her old house. "I've got to tell you. I may have to go away soon. There are big problems in the world. And I may be asked to do something about it."

"That is soon, but this is right now. Can't you give me some affection right now?"

"When you come on, you come on."

"Well, come on."

He took her in his arms and kissed her, and he meant it. She melted in his arms. He let her up.

She pulled her head back and gasped, "I don't know or care where you got that, but I want more." She dove in again. Several moments, she relaxed and reclined against his chest. "I would let you to my breast, but if I come out of this top, I'll never get it back on."

"I'll get along without it."

"I can let you have anything else. What do you want?"

"I want you to talk to me."

"What do you want me to do—talk dirty to you?"

"No. Just what you feel. What's in your heart? What do you like, or don't like? What do you aspire to be?"

"Now that might take the rest of your life."

"Are you trying to tell me something?"

"Maybe. What does *aspire* mean?"

"It is what you want to be or what you try to be."

"I can't tell you what is in my heart because I'm not that good with words."

"I like the early-morning sunshine after a good rain."

"I don't like to be without you."

"Because you are a woman, are you afraid of the pain of child birth?"

"No, because after birth and you hold that baby and nurse it, there is no thought of anything else. Mama says it is a feeling of euphoria."

"Why would you ask me such a question?"

"I just needed to."

"At least, that is what my mama said."

"I better get you home. Your mama might worry."

"She doesn't worry when I'm with you."

Peggy began inviting him over on the weekend mornings for her special breakfast, and Sunday dinner after church. She had to have it well-known that she would prepare every bit of them. During the summer, he would spend even more time at her place. Then toward the end of August, he received a notice to appear before a committee in Washington, DC. He could not tell anyone about his assignment.

He had to simply disappear. But Peggy remembered what he said after the Christmas formal.

He was sent to San Diego and received twenty-one injections. He was headed for the South Pacific and Australia but made his way to Singapore on a tramp steamer. He found that the Japanese were hooking up with the Germans in exchange of their engineering expertise in torpedoes. Because of having a short piquant with a German engineer's wife, he was able to spy on his secret papers. He made it appear that he was interested in a longer engagement but soon disappeared. He knew those drawings would be of great interest at Pearl Harbor. He tried to impress upon them the gravity of his information, but they were more interested in the question of what the Germans were doing in the Pacific.

He caught a B-17 heading to Moffett field and traveled commercial to Washington, DC, and debriefed. He bought a newspaper and read about Rommel invading North Africa. He thought of Greece and Corfu and those stunning young women he left in what could turn out to be harm's way. He caught a flight to Gibraltar, then a steamer through the Mediterranean, to the Adriatic Sea, and Corfu. He searched the fishing villages but found only three girls that he listed, and two of them were unwilling to leave their mothers. The one whose name was Abila, her mother died the year before, while hiding Abila from the German soldiers, so her father was anxious to get her out of the area. Jack took her to Gibraltar and acquired her papers that would allow her to stay in London. He stayed with her for a couple of weeks, but with the air raids, he decided to move to Liverpool.

While they were traveling, he learned a great deal of information about her. One of the most important things he learned was that she was studying English, being taught by Christian missionaries. She was still having trouble with pronouns, but with practice, they would come around. He took her to the US embassy, seeking a passport for her. That meant trips to London even though the Battle of Britton was still going on. On days in Liverpool, he would ask her questions about herself and what happened before the Germans came. He was hoping to give her experience putting sentences together. Because of overcrowding in the hotels of Liverpool, they were forced to share a two-bedroom flat. She became partial to long, warm showers and was not the least bit shy about asking to have her back patted dry. She also liked to have her long chestnut-brown hair detangled and brushed out. Jack was most obliging. He took the opportunity to get her to open up.

One early morning, he asked her, "You are a woman. What were you made for?"

She turned to the side. "I am not sure. Mama said that I was built for having babies, but how can I do that when I am not sure I will survive? I know I would need a husband to survive and have babies, but there is not a man for me. They all went fishing when they heard that the Germans were coming. I had a friend, but he was much younger than me. He would be my tail, but nothing more."

He lifted her hair and wiped her back. "What kind of man would you like?"

She pulled her towel from around herself and wiped under her bosoms, and drying her underarm hair, she turned to him. "I don't know, maybe one like you. You haven't whipped me one time. And I know I have made many mistakes."

"Do you believe that you must be punished when you make a mistake or disobey, so you will learn?"

She folded her towel and laid it across her lap. "My papa said, 'If you don't get a beating or being whipped, how would you know what you have done is wrong?'" She had an inquiring look on her face, but he would not answer. She stood up swinging her hair from side to side. "Will I get dressed now?"

He looked her up and down. "Yes, but we will go shopping for some more suitable attire for you."

"Does that mean that my dress is unacceptable?"

"No, it simply means that I want you to be in the style of the day, and that will call for some other undergarments, hose, garter belts, and a couple of brassieres. And of course, some new shoes. We will top it off with a couple of hats. A lady should never be seen outside without a hat."

"All the new customs, I suppose. I will just have to get used to it."

As they entered the shop, he said, "I will speak with your mistress."

The attendant replied, "As you wish, sir."

The mistress approached from the back of the store.

Jack confronted her. "I wish this young lady to be measured and attired in the current fashion, from toes to the top of her head. Treat her courteously, and don't be the cat. Do not say anything of a demeaning nature about her current attire."

The mistress replied, "Go behind the screen and disrobe. These will be hung in a garment bag. Hold your arms up, so I can measure your breast size, 36-D. Suck in your tummy. Waist, twenty-two inches; hips, thirty-eight. Bring two brassieres, white, 36-D."

"What are those for?" quipped Abila.

"So you will not begin to sag," answered the mistress.

At that, Jack stepped out to the lobby and stood waiting. In time, the attendant appeared carrying three garment bags and helped Jack get the bags into a waiting cab. They arrived at their flat.

Abila complained, "These are scratching me, and I feel bound up. May I remove this? It is like a horse's bridle. I feel restrained. And it feels as though it is cutting my flesh." She removed her blouse. "Will you help me with the hooks at my back? I can't reach it. It feels as though I might break an arm, trying to do that."

"Yes, and here is a nice little robe for you to wear around here, inside. Did you eat enough for lunch? I noticed you were a little constrained by the new clothes."

"I am still afraid most of the time. My stomach is in a knot, so many new things. I was really afraid on the plane. I prayed it would stay up."

He began to realize her education would take some time. She spent her entire life on that island, not realizing it was an island. She knew that the boats went fishing, but they always came back. And they ate the fish. From the window of the plane, she saw that the world was much more. She apparently lived in isolation for her first sixteen years.

"What will you miss the most?" he asked.

She stroked the lapel of her robe. "Fresh fish, every day. My papa, he, would cut for me the head of a big black fish. I would bite the cheeks off first and chew it very slow. Yummy."

"Is it not cooked?"

"No, fresh, raw, because it is fresh. It is better just fresh. Then the best is, I suck the eye of the fish out, and I would suck very hard. That way, I get the gray meat. Once the eye is out everything else, inside comes out, very tasty."

"You are eating the eye and the brain."

"Maybe, I think. It's good breakfast. Better than fried bacon."

At that point, he realized that he would have to get her acclimated to her new surroundings and culture. He thought of the winery and Erma. Abila just might fit in, and the area might allow her to ease into California life. Abila's passport finally arrived. He told her that she would not need a hat in America. She was still afraid, but he was able to coax her into one more ride in an airplane. Then it was New York and on to Denver because Chicago was snowed in. Finally, San Francisco, and a car to the vineyard. He told Erma that Abila's father retreated to northern Greece and, hopefully, would be able to follow Abila as soon as hostilities came to an end. Erma was happy to have a partner. He kissed and hugged them both and headed south.

*****

It was a good thing that he left at daybreak because it took him two hours to get from Sonoma to Lodi and hook up with Highway 99. He was hoping that he would not get stuck behind an Army convoy. As he crossed the bridge over the San Juaquin River, he felt, like he was home free. He would still have to go to the big city and come in on Sunset Boulevard To get back to his little town. He caught Woodside, off Sixth Street, and cruised up in front of their new house. He got out, striding to the other side of the car, and leaned against the front fender. There were children playing with a water hose on the grass of the front yard.

He stood there for a few minutes, then decided that something was not right. He stepped up on the sidewalk, and strode to the cement walkway that led to the front steps. At about halfway to the steps, the front screen door slowly opened. Mrs. Dobbs stepped out, holding the door open wide for him. He noticed tears in her eyes and a crumpled and soaked handkerchief in her hand.

He stumbled into the living room. "What has happened?"

She let the door close on its own, following him in. "We didn't know how to reach you because the meningitis took her so quickly. And the Health Department forced her to be sealed off from everyone because of fear of infection. We, they, didn't know where it came from or how it happened."

He tried to console her, but it was difficult, with tears streaming down his own cheeks. He hugged her, pressing her head against his chest. "If you need anything, please let me know."

She grasped his upper arms and leaned back. "We will be fine. You have helped more than we could ever repay. Thank you so much."

The children playing in the front yard had no idea what was going on in the house and had no need to know anymore, then what they already knew. He walked out on the front porch, looked down the street to the end at a cross street. He felt a deep loss. He knew that he would have to get out of that town, or he would fall apart. He hadn't determined his route, but he found himself cruising along on Highway 99.

He came to his senses, just before the turnoff to Gilroy. Something said, "This is the way."

He caught it, then up, and over Pacheco Pass. Through Gilroy and on to 101 North. San Jose, the little fruit packing town, then into Palo Alto, with Nicky to see. Nick and his two brothers welcomed him in and gave him solace and succor, and of course, they had to make it a party with a big barbecue and celebrate their brother's return.

*****

In the meantime, unbeknownst to them, Erma and Abila were working and having a serious discussion.

Erma came to the end of the vines, where Abila was cultivating the limestone soil. "Abila, put that hoe away for a while. I have something to tell you."

Abila stood leaning on the hoe handle. "Am I doing it wrong?"

Erma heard from Nick that Jack was with them, and there would be discussion about Abila, so she wanted to prompt her about Jack's bearings. Nick, also urged Michelle, to join in the discussion, and she was anxious to do so. She was waiting in the wine cellar, quite anxious to tell what she knew of Jack's character, and demeanor. From the moment they all came together, there was empathy and love all around.

Erma motioned for her to lean the hoe against one of the vines. "No, there is nothing wrong but come with me to the cellar. I have something for you."

As they walked along, Abila pulled off her gloves. "It is good that you suggested for me to wear these gloves. My blisters have almost healed."

"I should have told you to wear them before you got those blisters. I'm sorry. You are such a good worker." They stepped into the cellar.

They all introduced themselves to one another.

Michelle elaborated first. "I was on my way to do myself in. I had it all planned out when I got to Miami. I had plans to overdose on laudanum. It was the only way I could escape having been sold into prostitution. However, on the first day, I remarked that I wished that I could wash my feet, but my feet were probably too smelly and dirty that I didn't want to take off my shoes. Well, Jack took off his jacket, cufflinks, and his white shirt. Producing a basin of warm water, a washcloth, with soap, and he began washing my stinky feet, even in between my toes. I broke down sobbing that he humbled himself for me—a whore. At that point, he could have had any part of me he wanted, but he simply raised me up. It is because of him that I am where I am today—a very successful woman."

Erma stood up. "For me, he pulled me out of the jaws of terror and war. Then we traveled all over Europe, and he gave me solace and succor every minute and every mile. He made a vow, and he kept it. I knew I could trust him in any circumstance. If he had not displayed empathy for me, I would have wound up in real trouble. At that time in Europe, no one could be trusted. Money would buy a woman's soul, or she could be sold one piece at a time. If he asks you to share his life, grab that golden ring. He's a one of a kind."

Michelle piped up again. "Don't look a gift horse in the mouth."

"But what if he won't want me? I am so unlearned, and I am surely not sophisticated. And what do I have to offer?" quipped Abila.

Erma shifted in her chair. "Why do you suppose he left you with me? When he smells your sweat, you will understand."

"I have experienced his forbearance and his bearing. All the time we were together, he only acted as my benefactor. I would have allowed him many times, but he only did what I asked of him. His vow is an axiom. This is from the Greek, so I understand the meaning more. If he gives me a pledge, I will give one back. And it will be for all of me."

At the Green's house, J. R. said, "God has everything planned, it must not have been meant to be. His plans are true."

"It appears that Abila has been determined. Perhaps you should go see how it plays out?" Nick chortled.

"You could use our backyard and arbor for the ceremony. Just give us a heads-up when you need it," quipped J. R.

"You're not trying to push me into something, are yah?" Jack chortled.

They both chimed, "You know us better than that, don't you?"

"No, but I'll be back." He went through the gate. As he drove North on 101, he was considering just how he would approach Abila. Many things were swirling around in his mind. "Stop *it!* Just say what is in your heart. I am shutting you down, Brain."

Meanwhile, back at the cellar, Abila put her straw hat on and slid her gloves on. "I have two more rows to clean up." She climbed the stairs and went to the fields.

Later that afternoon, she ambled slowly to the toolshed to put up the hoe and a narrow-mouthed shovel. She would take her gloves inside because she didn't want to allow critters to crawl inside and greet her in the morning. She turned to head for the house but noticed the light showing from inside the wine cellar and heard voices. There were two voices, quite familiar, female voices, but one that was lower and a little husky. A man's voice for sure, but she thought she recognized it. But she questioned herself. Stepping forward, she grasped the ajar door, and pulling it to full open, she saw Michelle, Erma, and Jack staring at her.

She just looked at them aghast. "I better go wash up." But she stood still as though frozen in place.

"Young lady, I want you to come to me now," he commanded.

She looked around and pointed to herself.

"Yes, I am addressing you," he commanded again.

She started down the stairs to the cellar, taking off her straw hat, and clutching it to her bosoms. As she reached the floor of the cellar, Michelle and Erma skedaddled up the steps and disappeared.

He dropped down off the barrel he was sitting on and knelt on one knee. "Will you marry me?"

"Yes, are you pledging to me?"

"Yes, and here is your engagement ring." He slipped it on her finger.

She unbuttoned and slipped off her long-sleeved flannel shirt and threw her straw hat on the barrel. "You sit on the chair."

As he did, she slipped out of her brassier. She sat on his lap. "I'll have you smell my sweat. Won't that get something started?"

"Yes, but we will have somethings to talk over first. *Wow!* You are sweaty."

"And I am pliant, only for you. You are master, and I am your own," she confessed.

He only had a couple of things to bring up.

"What are the dates of your menses?" he questioned.

She backed away a little, looking puzzled. "I get a belly ache at the end of the month, but it's done by the end of the first week. What will that matter? You can't have me then. I don't think you will like it. What does the date of my menses matter?"

It was the middle of September.

"It just does," he quipped.

That meant that he should get the ceremony set up by the next weekend. The license was the first step and then to call Nick and J. R. They would arrange for the minister. He thought of a honeymoon in Hawaii.

*****

It was a private and quiet ceremony and a Clipper flight to Oahu and yada yada. They had a reservation for two weeks at the Hilton in Honolulu.

After a week of confinement in their suite, Jack chortled. "Don't you want to go to the beach?"

She laid on her back. "Can we make love on the beach?"

He pursed his lips. "The sand might cause a problem. Also, I'm not sure we could find a beach that would be secluded enough."

"It wouldn't be good in the salt water either. Maybe we will stay here. It's easy here."

The phone rang. Jack picked it up. "Hello, Blackwell."

The front desk answered, "You have guests waiting for you in the front lobby."

"Tell them I will be down in twenty minutes. Thank you," Jack quipped. "Abila, we must get dressed. I will meet someone downstairs in a few minutes."

"Okay, are we going home now? I am already pregnant anyway."

"How can you say that you are pregnant?"

"I know that I am. I felt it two nights ago. A woman knows this."

"Let's hurry and get dressed. This may be important."

Downstairs, the admiral met them as they stepped from the elevator. He was backed by two full colonels.

"Admiral Stars, who are your companions?" Jack quipped.

Stars shifted his feet. "Just a couple of advisors we had to track you down."

"Gentlemen, allow me to introduce my new bride, Mrs. Abila Blackwell." Jack forced the issue.

"Pleased to meet you, Mrs. Blackwell" Came from all three.

The admiral asked, "May we have a short meeting in your suite?"

"Fine," said Jack.

They all went upstairs. No secrecy was called for. They were simply assigning Jack to CINCPAC (Commander-in-Chief, Pacific Command). Jack would be able to take Abila to California on the next weekend. He wanted to be sure she would be close to a hospital. Then he would come back to Pearl to join the information crew. Something was in the wind. Britain also thought something was up. They were moving the *Prince of Wales* battleship to Shanghai.

Jack left Abila in the care of Michelle at Palo Alto. There was a hospital less than a mile away. Jack bought his first home then. He wanted to spend a couple of weeks getting Abila and Michelle acclimated and settled into the home and the area. There was furniture and appliances to buy; phone, power, and water to hook up and start. He hadn't had much free time to spend, making love to his new bride, and he wanted to teach her how to drive, but in mid-November at five thirty in the morning, the doorbell rang. Jack stumbled to the door, donning his robe as he went. Pulling the door open, he peeked out to see a Western Union man. Jack opened the door. By then, Abila and Michelle stood directly behind him, craning their necks around to see who was standing in the bath of the front- porch light.

The Western Union man asked, "John Blackwell?"

Jack answered, "I am."

"Please sign for the message." He handed the case to Jack.

Jack signed, and the telegram was delivered. Michelle, reaching around from behind Jack, handed the delivery boy a dollar.

Jack said, "Thank you." And he closed the door. Jack slowly and deliberately walked to the kitchen, flicking on the light switch as he entered. He took a seat at the kitchen table while Abila and Michelle stood, not knowing what to do. He glared at the envelope, then laid it on the table.

Looking up, he asked, "Why don't you girls take a seat?"

Michelle pulled a chair back but asked, "Should I make some coffee?"

Jack said, "No, not yet. I want you both to hear this." With that, he took the envelope from the table.

The girls were both sitting as he pulled the envelope open, unfolded the paper, and began to read.

It read:

Proceed to Moffett Field on November 22, 1940, at 5:00 AM.

Abila wrapped her robe around tight, folding her arms under her breasts, blurted out, "That is tomorrow. That is too soon. We just got started."

Michelle looked up, stuck out her chin, and said, "There is danger. He is needed. He will save lives, but I still pray he will come back to us."

They would have the rest of that day to share the love, just being with each other.

At four o'clock the next morning, Abila was sound asleep, and he tried not to wake her as he crept to the second bath, did his business, and donned his uniform. In the living room, he turned on the nightlight to make a phone call. He was calling for a military cab when Michelle brought him a hot cup of coffee as she turned on the light in the kitchen that shone into the living room. Then the whole room lit up as Abila switched on the living-room lights.

She stormed in wagging her finger, admonishing him. "Don't think you can sneak and creep out of our house without giving your wife a big wet kiss and a long two-minute hug, while I rub my bosoms all over you. So you don't forget what you have at home."

Michelle, backing toward the kitchen, almost whispered, "I'm just here. I made the coffee and brought a cup hoping to get a kiss and a hug goodbye."

Jack, facing off to Michelle, asked, "Come, give me a hug, and a kiss goodbye."

She complied but began sobbing. He pushed her back by both arms; he lifted her chin up to face him.

"I'm coming back, promise." He wiped her tears.

She turned and walked toward the kitchen.

Jack turned his focus to Abila. He pulled her to himself and kissed her long and deep. A horn honked outside.

He said, "That must be my ride. Don't come out. I'll be back." He pulled the door closed behind himself. He stepped off the porch, onto the cement walkway. One of the Gis got out and opened the backdoor of the sedan, and as Jack stepped into the light of the streetlamp that shone on his little front yard. The GI saw his number and saluted. Jack returned the salute and crawled into the back seat.

As he settled himself in, he asked, "Do you have any paper for me?"

The driver turned and said, "I doubt if you will get anything before you get to Hickam. He dropped the gearshift into second and didn't scratch a gear. One very good driver. They pulled into Moffett. The transport was already warmed up waiting in front of the large hanger. We pulled around behind the wing. A major stood at the bottom of the stairway. They booth climbed up and into the open door. Jack took a seat and looked out the window. He watched as the stairway was pulled away. After a short taxi and a swift liftoff, it seemed that they climbed, for what may have been five minutes. Then it was rattle and shake but only a few drops.

Then he went into Hickam, with almost no crosswind. On the ground, it was still dark, and he still had to get to the naval base at Pearl. He rode a jeep to a boat to another jeep. Watching daybreak at Pearl was spectacular. He stood at attention as the stars and stripes were raised. Then down into the depths of CINCPAC, three stories below.

# JAPONISME

Jack recalled his pre-bachelor degree. Basic knowledge classes included anthropology, which got him enamored, with Japanese culture and the language. He devoted two years to the language and became quite fluent in it. He found incidental quirks, most alluring, such as how Japanese mothers nursed their babies, with no bodily contact. They simply hovered over the baby, even the burping was done by the baby's grandmama.

Men between the ages of sixteen and thirty-five frequently developed esophagus cancer. The reason being that they were the first to sup soup or any other steaming hot liquids, scalding the lining of the esophagus and mouth. There were festivals celebrating the *phallus* in several mediums like candies on a stick.

The big turnabout came with Tokugawa Shogun, the restoration of the emperor. This was brought about by the visit of Commodore Perry in 1853 causing animosity toward the USA by the Japanese and prompted a military buildup in Japan. This all came about by the longing for coaling stations. Steamships made their daube. Sometime later, the Japanese defeated the Russians at sea. In the meantime, they had a running battle with Korea, for years.

Jack was gazing back down the hall; someone pushed the down button of the elevator. Somebody grabbed his arm and pulled him into the elevator. Nobody spoke. The elevator stopped when it hit the bottom. The doors creaked open.

The major said, "We usually take the stairs. They're safer."

Jack looked at a flickering light in the ceiling. "What is that smell?"

The major asked, "Jerry, what is that smell?"

"It could be sweaty socks, my underarms. I don't remember what a shower looks like."

"Tell me there is a toilet," he whimpered.

Jerry chortled, "Yes, and it is well vented to the surface with four stools, and I haven't counted the urinals."

"How many can translate Japanese into English?" asked Jack.

A tall, heavy man wearing a gray-and-purple sweater stepped forward. "There are three, including you. I'm Jasper. I have a star, but down here, that doesn't mean much, just success. We all work together for it. A transmission came in this morning. I want you to look at it and tell me what you think. You need to get into their mind and tell us what you think is going on."

He handed Jack a slip of paper. It came as a teletype and read:

> Six carriers are missing from Tokyo Bay. Just gone, disappeared.

Jasper said, "Our contact has been watching them for two weeks. Now they have vanished."

Jack stared intently at the scrap of paper. "Carriers are for carrying aircraft, and aircraft are for carrying bombs and torpedoes. They are going to attack but where?"

The answer would come in a couple of days with the sinking of the *Prince of Wales*. But there were only two Japanese carriers involved, and the port of Shanghai was demolished. Then they were spotted heading for Formosa, but where were the other four carriers? An Aussie in New Caledonia radioed that the Japs were moving through the Solomon to set up bases on New Guinea, looking at Australia. Solomon Islands and New Guinea were under attack. That would put Australia in jeopardy. US troops already sent a backup.

Japanese actions were underway in Dutch and French Indochina. They were in Hong Kong and in large tracks of mainland China. Four carrier groups disappeared. By the end of November, it had become a guessing game. An attack was coming but where? The first week of December, transmissions were coming heavy. Thankfully, the Navy had a decipher machine. They knew the Japanese code and were able to understand messages sent back and forth. On December 2, the commander of naval forces ordered the two carriers in port to take to sea and leave the support groups to stay behind because they were too slow.

At seven forty-five, Japanese planes appeared over Oahu, destined for Pearl Harbor, and the devastation of the US Fleet. It was December 7, 1941. By December 8, the harbor was nothing but smoldering wreckage. Back on the seventh, a squadron of B-17s flew right into the middle of the conflagration. The very next day, the Japanese lay siege to the Philippines. However, on April 18, 1942, the Doolittle Raid bombed Tokyo, taking the war to the Japanese. Apparently, it frightened the Japanese so that they wanted to enlarge their Coprosperity sphere to protect the home islands.

The Japanese began building up forces on New Guinea in an effort to make a move on Australia, so, the US sent two carrier groups to the Solomon and New Guinea to stop the Japanese advance. The *Lexington* was lost, but the *Yorktown* survived and limped back to Pearl and repaired within forty-eight hours—a usable ship to fight again at Midway. But that was in the future; with the war declared on Germany, the European front became the primary.

Jack and the group had been three-stories underground for nearly six months when the big break came. The Japanese messages displayed an interest in something they called F4. The identity was revealed when a radioman at Midway said on the open that their water purifier was broken. Soon, a message came from Japanese radio that F4 was out of water. So F4 was Midway, and that battle would change the war in favor of the USA. Island hopping and the battleship *Missouri* anchored in Tokyo Bay.

Jack sat looking at a poster of Rita Hayward wondering if his wife's hair was that long. He missed her so much.

Jasper stood next to him. "Are you feeling out of place yet?"

"Yeah, I've missed almost three years being with my wife. Would you believe I have a son? He must be almost three."

"How can you be so sure it's a boy?"

"Believe me, I just know."

"Whatever. It's time for you to get out of here. I have a slot waiting for you at Stanford if you want it."

"Really?"

"Yeah, let's go have a drink on it."

They caught a private ride sitting in a jeep out front of the building. Jasper commandeered him and the jeep; they had both donned their uniforms.

He the general said, "Downtown. The Shangri-La must be open by now."

A single scotch apiece, and they were on their way home. They raced the sun into Moffett field, and Jasper got another jeep and dropped Jack off at his house in Palo Alto, then went on to his home in Scott's Valley, just over the hill. Before he left, he reminded Jack to report at the tower on the Stanford campus, next Thursday. They said their goodbyes, and Jasper sped off.

Jack saw the Ford sitting on the driveway, thinking that Abila was waiting inside for him. He had his own key to the front door, but he thought he might surprise her. He pushed the button that rang the doorbell. He stepped expecting the screen door to swing out, but no response. He stood there bemused. He searched for his key, pulled it from his pocket. The key fit the lock okay. He pushed the door and stepped inside. Looking around, he found a small table close to the door with the phone and a writing pad. On the pad was the address of the farm up in Napa. He searched the house for any other clues; finding none, he determined he should go to the farm. The little Ford turned over quickly. He glanced at the gas gauge, noting that the gauge said almost full. He felt at ease. So off he went and over the bridge heading north. At the turnoff, there was a new mailbox. He followed the dusty road through the vines to the large stone building. There were trucks, and cars parked away from the building. He got out of the car and began walking toward a double door hanging on the door's header. A smaller door hanging on the large door opened, and Michelle stepped out.

She looked at Jack and shouted back through the door, "Abila, your man is here!"

He heard her yelling from inside. "Ba-ba-ba-baby!" She was out the door in a flash. She tore past Michelle and jumped, straddling Jack, and cried, "My baby, my lover, my sweetheart, my man, my husband came back for me."

Jack chortled. "Yes, I thought I would surprise you." He smelled her sweat.

"I have something for you," she shouted. "John Fitzgerald, come meet your daddy."

Little Jack toddled out, and his daddy picked him up.

There were hugs and kisses all around. Erma, Michelle, and Abila, even Nick, were there to help with the crush.

"The girls have been telling me how wonderful you are, but there is one that they don't know about, and that is, Tilly. Now this girl had gotten herself pregnant, and her father sent her to Hamburg, Germany, to get it aborted. Now the bawds were using a poison that would kill and abort the baby, but there were terrible side effects such as sterilization, even death, so he convinced her to keep the baby, so we set her up at Liverpool with a nice family. And what about the Jewish girls and families he saved?"

Jack asked, "Is the crush done?"

Erma quipped, "Yes, and we have been running since 1940, and we still have a 1943 that is very good. Would you like a glass?"

"Yeah, I'd like to try it. Oh, it's a cabernet!"

Nick chortled. "I'll take a glass, if you please."

Jack swirled his wine and said, "Can I take my family home now?"

Abila hung on Jack's neck. "I have a lot of catching up to do," she quipped.

Erma touted, "You two, go on. We will bring little Jack home in a day or two."

Abila and Jack headed for Palo Alto, and yada yada.

*****

The next Thursday, Jack was at the institute, but that would be the last workday of the week, a time for him to be introduced and acclimated to such a laid-back environment, but he also became aware of the cat. He had always been a voracious reader and even continued reading material on vinology during slack time at the winery. He kept his work at the institute under wraps and never expressed his views outside the meetings. Many of the secrets frightened him, but he stayed mum. Somehow, he was able to keep his work and his family separate, perhaps with the help of the time spent at the farm and the winery.

Furthermore, he had absolute knowledge of Christ Jesus and the mutual love between God and himself, which he shared with friends and family. This saw him through graduations, weddings, and twelve grandchildren. He retired from the institute, while he was still able to get around well and had some aspirations. Before he retired, they built a large covered and screened patio, with two firepits, for cool or wet rainy times. No need of air-conditioning in Napa. It faced west for the spectacular sunsets.

All his family and friends were assembled because the 1981 crush was finished. The 1977 vintage was passed around, and glasses were raised.

Abila held her glass high and asked, "John Blackwell, are you satisfied with what God has given you?"

"God has blessed me, and I am satisfied!"

The entire group raised their voices. "We are blessed because of you, Jack."

He was humbled and began to weep, but there was a smile on his weathered old face. And he did it all through his Lord Jesus Christ. Like he told Erma and Michelle, things done in the past were all in the past. Don't look back. Look ahead to Christ. God loves you and will forgive you. Find his truth through Christ.

# ABOUT THE AUTHOR

Dan Brizzee is a teacher, striving to never stop teaching; so he continues teaching through his stories.

559- 349- 7332
Dan

Printed in the USA
CPSIA information can be obtained
at www.ICGtesting.com
CBHW030521040824
12605CB00001B/93

9 798891 579316